THE WINE OF ASTONISHMENT

THE

WINE

OF

ASTONISHMENT

by

RACHEL MACKENZIE

B·O·O·K·S & Co.

A Turtle Point Press Imprint

New York

B·O·O·K·S & Co.
TURTLE POINT PRESS
New York

© 1974 by Rachel Mackenzie
Reprinted by arrangement with Viking Penguin,
a division of Penguin Books USA Inc.

Design and composition:
Wilsted & Taylor Publishing Services

Library of Congress Number 96-083495
ISBN 1-885983-17-4

Thou has shewed thy people hard things:
thou hast made us to drink the wine of astonishment.

PSALM 60

$\mathcal{R}$EMEMBER in the winter how she used to pour buckets of water on the walk in front of the house?" my sister asked when she was visiting me recently. She sat very straight in a hard chair, working on a piece of needlepoint, while I lay stretched out on a couch near the fire. We were talking over old times in a desultory sort of way. Wind blew pellets of snow against the windows with force enough that you could hear them strike.

No, I said, I didn't remember anything of the sort.

"Of course you do. You must!" My sister was impatient with me. "Whenever it was cold enough to freeze, there she'd be, out with her buckets of water, making a slide for us."

"But how could she? There were steps going up from the sidewalk. We'd have broken our necks."

"You're confused. The steps were at the porch. The walk sloped straight down from the bottom step to the street. It was a wonderful slide—that was a good steep pitch. I remember it absolutely."

"It's odd that I don't," I said.

She put in a stitch or two. "And remember the other one who wore those funny old bonnets—a different one each time?"

"I know you're wrong there," I said. "She only wore them once."

"That's not what I remember."

"You've stretched them out," I said. "Only the once. I know it for a fact." I am the older sister, which put her at a disadvantage.

My sister finished off the strand of pumpkin-colored wool she'd been using and looked up at me. "Well, whether you remember it or not, I'm sure about the slide," she said. "We passed that house on the way to school. In winter, I looked every day, hoping." And there we let the matter rest.

I've searched and searched, but I cannot find that slide anywhere in my memory. It seems a large thing to have lost—and then it gives me an uneasy feeling that my sister and I may have been living separate lives during our childhood when all this time I have thought we lived one.

1

THE OLD Henderson house was a landmark in Pliny Falls—one of those Greek Revival, plumply pillared houses that grace small towns through upstate New York. Elm trees bordered the walk in front, feathering out in summer to form with the trees across the way a high, cool arch over Main Street, and at one corner of the wide yard a copper beech glowed against the soft gray of the house and the immaculate white of the pillars and shutters. There were lilacs in the back yard, and a grape arbor, and an old cherry tree that still bore fruit. In winter, the house stood warm and foursquare in its dressing of snow, with a larch tossing great sweeps of shadow

3

over its face. It was a handsome house, handsomely set, just enough farther back from the street than any of its neighbors, on just enough of a rise of ground, to give the impression of overlooking and dominating the village.

From inside, Emmeline Henderson overlooked and dominated, too—straight up until the day in early March when she died abruptly of a stroke. "I've given my *life* to my girls!" was the way Emmeline Henderson put it. She had. At least she hadn't married again after the death of her young husband back in 1890, and the two little girls were what she had left—the little girls and the Henderson Preserving Company; she had that. Martha and Esther. Bible names. Hendersons were the backbone of First Presbyterian Church. The stained-glass, pink-cheeked, purple-robed Christ kneeling in a clump of iris high above the sanctuary had the Henderson name on it, and a good deal that went on in the session might have if there'd been any reason to give it a label. Ownership of Henderson Preserving Company carried its responsibilities. Pliny Falls hadn't grown to plan after the Canal dwindled as a waterway. First Presbyterian stayed the first and only, and over the years Henderson's stayed the village's single large prospering industry.

4

No other children in the Sunday School had beaver hats with brims so wide or streamers down their backs so far over their long, crimped hair as Martha and Esther Henderson. No other children had so many private lessons, going to Syracuse and Auburn to take them—Piano, Elocution, Voice—or, as a result, performed in public with so many gestures and so much aplomb. And no other children spent so much time with their mother. "My girls are delicate," she said. "They've always been sheltered. They're young for their age. And I want to keep them that way as long as I can. With me. Young and innocent and sweet."

Esther went away once, the summer after she finished high school. With a godlike young man the Masons had hired to put on an Entertainment—the final number was a wedding, with the parts all acted out by the men. But she didn't get very far. Her mother caught up with her in Rochester. "In time, thank God!" was as much as she ever said, and she brought Esther back. Anything else said on the subject was not said in the Henderson presence. The only change in Esther so far as you could see was that she set herself at more of a distance from other people than she had before; she'd always been aloof. Temperament—that was the word for Esther. The young man had been a Catholic, to boot. There was never any trouble with Martha. Esther was the high-spirited one—the pretty one, the favorite.

As they were considered to have grown up and vacancies made room, the girls followed their mother into Tuesday Club and Friday Club, and they joined the Delphian Course—and Women's League at church, naturally. Martha had played the organ there for years, and Esther sang in the choir. "We keep busy enough!" they'd tell you with a laugh. And time hardly touched them. They had a fresh-skinned, uncertain quality that made them seem years younger than they were, and they were given to small, girlish ways and ribbons in their hair.

Martha was thirty-two and Esther twenty-nine that cold March day their mother died. She was clearing out the tulip beds with the same vigor she'd used all her life to attack dirt—or wrongdoing—or opposition—when she toppled forward into the half-rotted leaves she'd raked into a pile.

Rebecca Daniels saw it happen from her back yard next door. She was hanging out her wash. It was washday up and down the village—Monday, with a spanking breeze and the promise of sun later on. She let the sheet she was pinning drop to the ground and ran over, ducking under the low branch of the cherry tree that grew near the property line, puffing. Rebecca had high blood pressure. She brushed the leaves from Mrs. Henderson's aristocratic, fine dead face and looked furtively over her shoulder toward the house. There was no sign that anyone had seen; she'd have to go for the girls. She took a step, hesitated, came back. Untying her apron, she spread it over Mrs. Henderson's head and chest. Bluing had dribbled down one side and a big patch in the center was dark with wash water, but she left it, the ties lying as haphazard as Mrs. Henderson's own feet in their oxfords, as the rake that had fallen from her hand.

Rebecca thanked the Lord that Martha was alone. You could count on Martha to hold up. But Esther, down at Dr. Kinney's having a tooth filled, couldn't get over not being there. "He kept me waiting!" she sobbed when she'd run the four blocks home, wild-eyed, her coat clutched in front of her. "If he hadn't kept me waiting, I'd have *been* here!"

Martha put her arms around her. "It wouldn't have made a bit of difference, Esther honey. I was in the basement, starting the first tub to rinse—that close—and I never knew a thing was wrong. Rebecca had to come find me."

Esther pushed her away. Her eyes smoldered,

great dark eyes set so deep you were conscious of their sockets—like her mother's eyes, except that Esther's flickered this way when the current of her feelings ran too strong. "*I'd* have known. When he came away from the telephone and said, 'You must be brave, Esther, I have bad news for you,' I *hated* him! Knowing something before I did and daring to keep it from me like that!"

Esther was difficult, no question of it. "No! No! No!" she shouted as Dr. Phipps and Rebecca and Martha carried Mrs. Henderson in through the side door and laid her on the couch in the little room the girls called the den but that she had always called the office because the roll-top desk there was consigned to business correspondence and records from the company. They covered her with an afghan. Esther wouldn't even see it. She paced around the dining-room table, shouting "No!" and every time she said it she struck the table with the flat of her hand. Dr. Phipps had to give her a hypodermic. He and Rebecca took her upstairs, and after a while she grew quiet. Dr. Phipps shook his head when he came down, but into space. Martha wasn't there to see him. She sat out by the blanket-covered figure, folded over on herself in the old Morris chair.

"Shall I call Berryman for you, Martha?" Dr. Phipps's voice was dry and noncommittal. He felt it, though; he and Mrs. Henderson were near an age. He'd known her since she'd come to Pliny Falls, a bride. Close to forty years.

Martha nodded without lifting her head. So Dr. Phipps had Elsie Andrews at the telephone exchange get him the general store. Mr. Berryman did undertaking on the side. It was good having someone you knew look after your dead like that. "Ah, Martha, we're all made sad by *this*," Mr. Berryman said when he and Dick Pollock came, and it didn't seem so professional, turning her mother over to people who knew who and what she had been.

"Those girls are going to be *lost* without their mother!" Rebecca Daniels said across the back fence to Mrs. Beers. Mrs. Beers was feeding her chickens. It was a good place to see what was going on, and a decent excuse. "Mark my words!" Rebecca said. She had just finished telling how she'd rushed next door to find Emmeline Henderson stone dead alongside her tulip bulbs. Rebecca pressed her hand to her heart. "Gone to glory!" she said of what the shock had done to her own blood pressure. "She gave up

9

her *life* to those girls! She's said as much to me herself, many's the time. 'Rebecca, I've given up my *life* to my girls!' Many's the time I've heard her."

"A remarkable woman," Mrs. Beers agreed. "Always knew what she wanted." She threw out a handful of corn. "There's Hank again. More flowers. Must of come on the bus."

"There'll be flowers—you can count on that!"

"I guess money isn't everything, Rebecca." Mrs. Beers turned her pan of feed upside down. "No more. It's gone," she said to the chickens clucking away at her feet. "Poor things."

Rebecca pulled her old brown sweater together across the bulge of her breasts. "Oh, well," she said, rather apologetically, "love takes people funny ways. You have to remember they were all she had left, he died so young."

2

A PARADE of custards and casseroles and baked goods under shiny damask napkins made its way across the Henderson back yard. And callers! You could tell them half the length of Main Street by the Sunday hats and gloves, the dignified reluctance of their pace.

Esther waited just inside the hall. She had on black up to her chin, and her copper-colored hair was piled high on her head in a coronet of braids. Underneath them her face looked fragile, like fine china—as if, maneuvering it against the light, you could see shadows through. Her eyes were uncomfortably reminding.

"Good evening," she said. "Would you like to go in and see my mother?"—as composed and remote as the figure lying in the bronze casket before the long, shuttered windows of the drawing room. Too remote. No one could intrude on that with anything intimate or let tears escape before it. They were offered to Martha at the drawing-room door. "A sad loss. One of our landmarks gone," was the most that got said to Esther. Something about her made everyone feel self-conscious.

"Calling Mama a landmark! As if she was this house!" Esther said to Martha later. They couldn't seem to get themselves to bed. They roamed the downstairs rooms and sat for hours in the kitchen drinking tea while wind rattled the outside shutters.

Martha rested her head aginst the palm of her hand. Her head throbbed all along her fingers. "Mama and this house—our whole life, have you thought of that? Except for church, of course."

"I'll never be warm here again," Esther said, and she started to cry. "What are we going to do, Marty?"

Martha pulled herself up. "Let me light the oven for you." The gas exploded with a dull pop. "I expect we'll do what we've always done," she said. "After all, we still have each other."

"And we won't have to give up the house?" Esther's voice was muffled. "Because if we ever had to leave this house, I think I'd die."

Martha could not have got through without David. David Rathbone had been the minister at First Presbyterian for six months, a short enough time that feelings about him were unsettled. He was younger than the parish was used to—only forty—and then he had no wife and showed it. The cuffs of his shirts were ragged where he'd trimmed off the fraying, or neglected to, and more often than not his wiry black hair hung ragged over his collar. He seldom looked clean-shaven, his beard grew so fast. A plain man. Medium height. Good and honest and forthright— his face and his eyes made that clear—but plain. Mama said the first time she saw him it was background; his bones weren't fine, for all she admired him as a preacher. Mama judged by the bones. David's bones had strength, though. Everything about him was strong, chin, mouth, the set of his shoulders, his handshake. Even his hair went its own way, aggressively, in cowlicks.

David had walked into the Henderson house without so much as knocking, as if where sorrow waited was his home. When Martha saw him, a shower of tears escaped her. "It was so sudden," she explained then in a shaky voice. "I'm just not prepared."

He'd taken her hands in his and held them tight. "'What man is he that liveth and shall not see death?'" he'd said in the intimate, low voice he used when he passed the silver chalice to his elders at Communion. "'Shall he deliver his soul from the hand of the grave? . . . As for man, his days are as grass; as a flower of the field, so he flourisheth. For the wind passeth over it and it is gone; and the place thereof shall know it no more.' Do you know your Psalms, Martha?"

Martha clung to his hands. The everlasting arms, she thought. The everlasting arms.

David conducted the funeral service, his voice resonant and deep and full of comfort. But is was old Dr. Westcott's words that comforted Esther. They'd asked him to come back to deliver the eulogy because he'd been their pastor for so many years before he retired in the fall and it seemed more fitting to have a person their mother's own age speak for her life in the end. "*David*!" Esther said scornfully. "What does he know of Mama!"

Dr. Westcott said he had come to lay a little flower on the casket of his friend, and he looked down and cried. Then he drew on his faith to explain that this was only a separation, and in his papery voice he delivered a lengthy argument demonstrating the immortality of the soul.

And Oliver and Lucy Bradley sang. Oliver and Lucy lived across the street from the Hendersons—best friends, really; they ran in and out of each other's houses. Esther would have preferred just Oliver. He took all the tenor solos in church; his voice was not very big but it was mellow and sweet, and everybody liked to hear him sing, he could go so high without its seeming any effort. He and Esther cared for music in the same deep way. Esther felt shaken all the way through whenever she sang herself, she said. She couldn't abide music without feeling. It was what she held against Lucy—as a singer, that is. Soprano, like Esther. Her voice was true—Esther had to admit that; it was a good strong chorus voice—but it lacked feeling. She gave in, though, when she saw how much Martha wanted Lucy and Oliver together; they made a specialty of duets. They sang "The Old Rugged Cross" and "Abide with Me."

Afterward, Lucy sent over their supper, on a tray set with her Haviland, prettied up with a paper doily under the rolls, to look tempting—and Lucy hated to fuss. Oliver carried it. With his red-blond hair and his dapper mustache, Oliver brought something bright with him, even into this sad house. He came round to the back door, through the pantry, and when he'd put the tray down on the kitchen table he flicked off the towel that covered it and draped it over his arm like a waiter, and while Martha made tea he pulled out a chair for Esther, drawing it across the linoleum with a ridiculous flourish. For all that his eyes were full of sympathy, he acted like a clown, as he often did at choir rehearsal, and Esther couldn't keep from smiling. He sat and chatted and coaxed them into eating Lucy's salmon loaf with egg sauce, which she had fixed because she knew that Martha was especially fond of it.

Then Oliver left, and there they were. Esther pushed away her plate and stood with such violence that the chair crashed back onto the floor. "I can't bear it!" she said in a desperate, charged voice. "Let's go to the cemetery!"

"The cemetery!" Martha stared up at her.

Without a sound, Esther began to cry. Fat tears rolled down her face. "You've got to understand," she said. "I feel so lost."

The cemetery was half a mile to the north of town

off the country road into which Main Street ran, on a hillside that in summer would be pleasant enough, with oak and maple and elm a sheltering canopy over the graves, the last thread of the outlet, willow-lined, trickling past at the foot. But in March it was a gray, bleak place, and the outlet rattled along with the rough urgency of spring on its way. The family plot was on the highest level, and the granite shaft marking it pointed the Henderson dead a yard or so nearer Heaven than any in the neighboring graves. HENDERSON was cut deep into the face of the block on which the shaft rested, and around the other three sides there ran in smaller, slanted letters, "He leadeth me beside the still waters." With the outlet making all that commotion below! The funeral flowers were already shrinking in the cold, damp air; the wires that bound them into wreath and cross and sheaf showed through, and between the pieces moist, brown earth. Martha's eyes burned with tears.

Esther never looked off the ground. "It's a peaceful place, isn't it." She sighed with relief. "I feel close to her again. It doesn't seem so final here."

The next evening it was the same. Then every evening. As soon as supper was over. After two or three times, Martha gave over protesting; it made Esther cry. The only person she mentioned it to was Lucy. "I

don't know what people must think," she said one
morning when Lucy had run over for a minute and
Esther was off to the post office to pick up the mail
from the box. "Why, we don't even stop to do the
dishes, and you know what Mama would have said to
that!"

Lucy rubbed the back of her hand up over her
forehead in a way she had. "Well, after all, it's nobody's business but your own, is it?"

"It's Essie. She says it helps her. She takes everything so hard."

"Hmph!" Lucy pursed her mouth. She had a thin,
intense face—tan. It merged into the color of her
hair. "Only I'd not let her keep me from redding up
my dishes first if I wanted to. I've got to get back. I
left Teddy minding Bud, and you know what that
means."

No one came out and said anything to the girls.
They weren't much bothered by callers, not after
they'd ushered a few into the drawing room, made
them feel like company. The two of them sat forward
on their chairs, polite but standoffish. Silences fell
and stretched awkwardly. For three weeks they
didn't even go to church. "It would bring it all back,"
Esther said. "I can't—just don't ask me." So much to
do, they were at pains to explain, that they had to do

alone: personal things like Mama's clothes to sort through and air pack carefully away in the old round-topped leather trunks in the attic—a last layer to the strata preserved over the years, and the trunks as good as the day they'd been bought, not a scuff mark on them.

And then there were the business things involving the estate. Their mother's will had set up a board of directors to run the factory: Martha and Esther; Sid Corbett, the manager; Mr. Latham, the family lawyer; and a second laywer, Mr. Dowling—practically a stranger—from Rochester. The votes on the board would be equal, but the girls between them held seventy-five per cent of the stock. It meant long sessions in the den, with Mr. Latham presiding from the roll-top desk. Miss Piper, the company's secretary, provided the figures and reports, but the girls had to attend while Mr. Latham went through them page by page, column by column, explaining.

And then there was the annual celebration of spring cleaning to be observed. Martha and Esther made a retreat of it, according to their mother's ritual, from attic methodically down and out the cellar. Every self-respecting woman in Pliny Falls was doing the same, and what with spring thrusting up outside, and inside all this exorcising of dirt, it didn't much matter that the Henderson girls continued to visit the cemetery the minute they had their dishes out of the way.

"It'll take time," Rebecca Daniels said philosophically across her back fence to Mrs. Beers, and Mrs. Beers said, "It's a good thing they *got* it!" But no one paid much attention until the night they took the birthday cake with them.

That was Esther's idea. "You haven't forgotten what day this is, have you?" she asked when Martha came down to a kitchen filled with sun and the sweet, thick smell of browning sugar and of coffee and the fresh wax they'd put on the floor only the night before. Esther was bent over the oven.

Martha looked at the litter on the kitchen cabinet and she tightened. "Of course I haven't. It's Mama's birthday. What of it?"

"I'm baking a birthday cake. I've been up since five."

"Oh, Essie!"

Essie closed the oven door carefully. "There's no use your 'Oh, Essie'ing me," she said coldly. Her mouth, which a second before had been round and smiling, drew down thin. From all the voice practicing she did, Esther's mouth was so mobile it was hard to keep up with the speed of its changes. Then she smiled again. "Caramel layer—Mama's favorite. I thought we could take a picnic and go to the cemetery early." Her voice grew soft with coaxing. "Why shouldn't we make a little party if we want to, and the house cleaning done and out of the way? What's the harm?"

"It's morbid," Martha said. "That's the harm—and whatever will people think! People are working on their plots, don't forget. It's spring, after all. Don't fool yourself there isn't plenty of talk already about our being up there every night."

"If you're going to let what people *think* . . ." Esther went to the window above the sink. "Look!" she said after a bit. "You can see the buds on the tulips." Martha had poured her coffee and carried it to the round table in the big south window before Esther turned back to the room. "I guess I'm like Mama," she said. "I'm going to live my own life, people can think what they choose. And if feeling Mama is close to me, as if I could *speak* to her—if that's *morbid*!" She flushed deeply. "I don't see how you can say such a thing. Your own mother!"

So they went, with sandwiches and a thermos of coffee, and the cake carefully packed in a hatbox, birthday candles in their holders set into the thick, rich frosting. And once they were there it seemed natural enough—a steamer rug spread out to sit on and an old maple to lean against, its red-flecked new leaves so quiet they hung like veiling overhead. As the day began to taper off toward evening, Esther lighted the candles. They wavered and smoked and rocked. "Quick! Make a wish before they go out!" she cried.

"I have," Martha said. Then she laughed—a hearty laugh into the fading light of the cemetery. "Remember that angel food we baked for Mama's birthday when we were little and it never rose above an inch high? Like a piece of bath sponge in your mouth, and we chewed away, and Mama said how good it was, and you burst into tears?"

Esther laughed, too, but she said quite soberly, "I never could stand it if things didn't turn out the way I'd planned."

Mrs. Beers had just fed her chickens next morning when Rebecca came by on her way to the Henderson house with a plateful of molasses cookies. "Cake!" Mrs. Beers threw out her hands. "Over their own mother's grave!"

"Candles!" Rebecca said.

"It's not wholesome, that's what it is—desecratin' the cemetery. Why, next thing you know they'll be out there in the dead of night, conjurin' her up to eat with 'em. I don't know what that poor woman would of made of such goin's on."

"She'd of made what any practicing Christian would make, and I said as much to David Rathbone this morning. 'If ever there was a place for the church to step in, Reverend,' I said, 'it's here.' I told him straight out it was up to him, and those girls carrying on like a pair of heathen, shutting themselves away, toting cakes to the grave—lighting candles. And I wager I wasn't the only one." She tipped her head to Mrs. Beers and went on next door with her cookies.

David dropped by in time to eat them. He didn't speak of the cemetery, but he stopped Esther when she made an excuse to go off, and he talked to them firmly about coming back to church. "Even though you feel you don't need us," he said, "if you had sat through the music these last weeks you would know how badly we need you. I want you to sing a solo for me Sunday, Esther. And Martha, I want to see you at the organ. I've missed you. Will you?"

Martha looked at Esther. Esther looked ahead—toward David but beyond him. "I'm awfully out of practice," she said at last, "but if Marty will, I will. I'm just beginning to realize—why, I wonder if that isn't partly what's been wrong with me: I haven't

23

been singing. Music matters more to me than anything else in the world—now, at this particular time,
I know it as I never knew it before."

Lucy ran over later. She brought a loaf of homemade bread and said it was time they put all this fool-
ishness aside. She was expecting them for supper—
she had a kettle of chili on the stove—and they could
go along with her and Oliver afterward to choir rehearsal. Oliver said to tell them if they didn't show up
he'd come transport them bodily. "The very idea!"
Esther said and laughed, and Martha said, "I don't
know," in a yielding voice, and Lucy said, "He meant
it!" and she wasn't taking no for an answer. She ran
off—Lucy was always on the run, like a mechanical
toy wound tight—before they could say another
thing, though they had only to look at each other to
accept that they'd kept themselves to themselves
long enough. It would be a relief to be out once
again.

3

ON SUNDAY, Esther sang "Oh, for the wings, for the wings of a dove" high and clear, and Oliver, watching from the other side of the choir loft, whose stalls faced each other across the chancel, thought that she looked ethereal in her black choir robe with its starched white collar. "Far away, far away would I fly!" she sang. With her copper hair burnished and her face as pale as a shell, she looked fragile and somehow purified, and Oliver's mind stumbled into the word "adorable." Esther cried through the prayer that followed her solo, and he thought how little she was and how defenseless against the pressure of emotion she contained. It was all he could do to keep from going to her, across the choir loft in the middle of the prayer.

At First Presbyterian, a hymn followed the sermon. The choir stood in place through the first stanza, then, singing, recessed up the aisle down which it had come earlier to open the service. The Amen was sung when the benediction had been pronounced from the pulpit, and the choir members, no longer in line, might linger to talk with friends in the congregation before making their way to the room in the basement where the gowns were kept, and the music, to put on their outdoor clothes.

That Sunday, Oliver waited for Esther downstairs, and when she came he gripped her arm hard. "You sang like an angel," he said. "I was afraid you might take off before I got to tell you how important it is for you to stay."

"Important?" Esther said in a dazed voice, and her eyes looked dazed, as if she *had* been far away and he had pulled her back.

"Don't you know that if you weren't here it would be like a light gone out?"

"Why, Oliver, I had no idea you cared so much for my singing." Esther stood stock still, staring up at him.

A note of bewilderment crept into his voice. "I didn't know myself," he said, and he moved his hands to rest them in a tentative gesture on her shoulders.

Though the basement was hot and stuffy, Esther felt herself shivering against his hands.

Martha's step on the old wooden stairs pushed them apart. Oliver touched his fingers to his mustache. Esther gave herself a little shake. "That song must have put a spell on me," she said in a light, breathless voice, and she walked away from him, swaying, over to the rack to hang up her gown.

"Well," Martha said as she opened the music cabinet and stooped to put away her volume of *Organ Melodies*, "and where's Lucy this morning? Not sick, I hope."

The spell was broken.

"No, no, she's all right," Oliver said. "It's Teddy. We're afraid he may be coming down with the measles."

"Oh, too bad," Martha said. "I hear there's a lot of it around. Tell her I missed her."

"I'll do that."

Martha straightened up from the cabinet. "Essie," she said, "I don't know when you've been in better voice. I was quite affected."

27

"I was just telling her she sounded like an angel," Oliver said. He touched his mustache again.

Esther threw her arms around Martha and kissed her. "I know I felt every note of it, if that's any test," she said.

"The best test in the world," Oliver said. "If there's anything I can't stand it's a cold singer. 'Get more *feeling* into it!' I keep saying to Lucy. She can't seem to let herself go—afraid, I guess."

"Tell her I'll try to get over to see her this afternoon," Martha said. She put her gown on a hanger.

Esther walked to the mirror; she studied herself, this way and that.

Oliver followed her. "Do that," he said over his shoulder to Martha. "And Esther, why don't you come along and we could try out that new soprano-tenor arrangement I've got for 'How Beautiful upon the Mountain.'"

"I thought you and Lucy were working that up," Martha said.

"We were, but it's too high for Lucy."

"She sounded all right the time I went over it with you."

Oliver shook his head. "Her voice keeps getting lower," he said. "Every time we have a child, it drops. It's been quite a problem since Bud—I've had to

28

carry her on the high notes. Her upper register's about gone."

Esther moved from the mirror. "How terrible for her!" she said. "And I'd love to, it's one of my favorites. Only . . ." She hesitated. "Only I was planning to go to the cemetery this afternoon."

Almost involuntarily, Oliver reached out toward her. "Still taking it so hard? He made his face sad. "Well, the way I look at it, if it's any help to you to be at the cemetery, let the busybodies mind their own business—you *go*. 'Leave her alone,' I've said to a couple of them. 'Quit picking on her.'" He gave her arm a squeeze.

"Marty doesn't think it's right, not really." Esther looked at him with her eyes wide.

"Not 'right,' exactly," Martha said from the foot of the stairs. "'Wise.' I think it only keeps reminding you to be sad."

Esther sighed. "It isn't like that at all. I can't seem to make anyone understand. It gives me strength to go on."

"I think *I* understand," Oliver said slowly, his hand still on Esther's arm. "I remember how it was when my mother died. I was only a kid. I used to sneak off to the closet under the stairs and just lean against an old tweed coat she wore out in the garden

29

and to run down to the store—an old thing like that, but it gave me a feeling I'd been around her for a minute."

Esther nodded.

"I guess maybe we both take things harder than ordinary people," Oliver said. "It's hard for them to understand. Look, Esther, why don't I go along with you this afternoon—I'd be glad to, and it would save Martha going. Unless I'd be butting in."

"Oh, you wouldn't ever do that," Esther said.

"My daffies are out. How about if I pick a nice bunch and bring them along—four-thirty, say? Sunday afternoon belongs to the boys—you know Lucy!—but that ought to work. Then Martha can run on over to the house and afterward we can all have a snack and maybe in the evening some singing."

"I'd like that," Esther said. "I really would. Would it be all right with you, Marty?"

"Why, of course." Martha started up the stairs. "And I certainly think it's nice of you to bother, Oliver," she said. "I don't know what we'd do without you and Lucy."

Martha had a curious sense of something beginning. It was as if she had suddenly come into a place of her own that she hadn't had before. A dozen members of

the congregation had waited in the vestibule to tell
her how good it was to have her back. They held on
to her when they shook her hand. Martha's eyes filled
with tears, but only because pleasure welled in her so
high. Out of her pleasure she turned to David. "Do
you have any plans for dinner?"

"Not up to this point," he said, smiling.

"Well, you have now. You're coming home with
us. Isn't he, Essie?" she asked as Esther appeared at
the head of the basement stairs.

And Essie had been generous. "He is if he'll do
us the honor." There was still that air of exaltation
about her. "I don't know what Gus was thinking of
yesterday," she said. "We've got a roast practically
the size of the oven."

"Man-size," Martha said, and laughed.

She laughed straight through the meal. Esther
went upstairs to lie down as soon as they reached
home. Martha insisted; she seemed feverish. Besides,
there wasn't much to be done. Sunday dinner, out
of habit, was prepared before the girls got into their
church-going clothes: the table set, the vegetables
peeled and put to soak. The roast would be in the
oven before they left the house.

"Make yourself at home!" Martha said to David
once coats were hung in the big closet off the hall.

She waved him toward the den, but he followed her to the kitchen and sat down in the old wooden rocker, whose seat was softened with a braided-rag-rug cushion. When she had the vegetables on and lifted the roast from the oven, he came over and cut a piece off the end, to try. She had placed it on top of the stove, covered with a towel to keep warm while the juices set, and he stood beside it, snipping away. Martha was delighted. "You're hungry!" she said, and she brought him a homemade roll spread with jam.

"I'm always hungry after a sermon. Delivering the word of God seems to empty the stomach. But I had no idea you were such a good cook." He speared a pickled pear from the cut-glass relish dish Martha had just filled. "Martha, you're hiding your candle under a bushel," he said. "You ought to be married!"

Martha was already flushed from the heat of the oven, but she felt her skin burn up into her hair and out to the tips of her ears. "I'm afraid it's a little late for that."

"*Late!*" David said. "What are you talking about?" After a slight pause, he added, "My dear."

The words were spoken casually enough, but the pause set up a vibration that sounded in Martha's mind long after he had left. She couldn't keep herself from mentioning it to Lucy when she went across the street. The boys were outdoors playing; Oliver and Esther had gone off to the cemetery.

"Well, I hope you're going to do something about it," Lucy said in her decisive, practical voice. "You can have David Rathbone if you want him, Martha. The only thing is, it's going to take some work. Any normal man who's got this far without marrying more than likely thinks of it as a trap. Or temptation."

"He's had to take care of his mother." Martha's tone was defensive. "She was in an old-ladies home for years, with arthritis. He was devoted to her. He told me all about it this afternoon. You'd know he'd be good to his mother, wouldn't you."

"You'd hope so, anyway," Lucy said. "And I expect she helped it along. But what I'd like is to see him devoted to you." They were sitting in the dining room. She pulled her chair up to the table and planted her elbows on the crocheted border of the rumpled cloth. There was a spot that looked like gravy in the center, and something more solid had been spilled near the edge. "It's time you faced up to a few things. You're not getting any younger, for all that you don't show it yet, and the chance of another man coming along in our lifetime—well, you've known this place

RACHEL MACKENZIE

longer than I have. Now your mother's gone and you're free at last—"

"Oh, Lucy," Martha protested, "don't put it like that. We miss Mama so."

"Of course you do. She absorbed you."

"But she was such a wonderful person. And besides, there's Essie."

"Essie! You don't need to worry about Essie! For heaven's sake look after yourself for a change."

Martha picked at the crochet in front of her.

"You'd make him an ideal wife," Lucy said, "only be careful you don't turn into such a help he starts thinking of you as an assistant minister. He already knows you can do church work, try to remember— the last thing you want is for him to be grateful. And give him a chance to see you without Essie always being around. You'll never get anywhere if every time he comes to see you he goes away with the idea he's made another call on the bereaved." She cocked her head, assessing. "You have a soft look, as if you'd be nice to touch. Sunday's probably your best bet to have him alone. Invite him to dinner a lot, the way your mother used to have the Westcotts. That's a family tradition. Nodoby will think anything of it. Afterward, Essie can come over here. Oliver won't mind walking her to the cemetery. It'll be good for

34

him, get him out—I'll take care of *that*. You've got everything to work with. That beautiful house. It's the one thing I envy you." She looked around the small, untidy, low-ceilinged room. "Sometimes it seems as if there wasn't space enough for a good deep breath in our whole downstairs, especially since Oliver went and bought the baby grand. I can't seem to keep things off it—Oliver gets after me—and I hate to see it all scratched up myself, before it's even paid for. Of course he wouldn't really have it any different. Whenever I do get things slicked up and put away he claims he feels as if he didn't live here any more. Men never know what they want." She shook her head. "You shouldn't have any trouble. Just being in love is the best help of all."

Martha stared between the rounds of the bird cage in the little bay window, where Billy, the canary, staring back, was as bright-eyed and quizzical as Lucy, his head cocked to one side at the same questioning angle. "I've never thought a lot about marriage," she said slowly. "About being married myself, that is. I've never had occasion to. But if . . . if you think . . . I suppose it would be what I want."

"Of course it is. You're just finding it out late. That's the whole trouble with you—you and Essie both. You never were allowed to grow up." She pushed herself away from the table. "Come on, run over 'How Beautiful upon the Mountain' with me. I'd like to surprise Oliver. There are a couple of places where he says I don't have the rhythm right, and he gets irritable with me."

"Would you like me to transpose it?" Martha asked as they walked across the narrow hall into the living room. "Oliver happened to mention that this arrangement was high for you."

"Nonsense," Lucy said. "I had a cold in my throat for a part of the winter. Oliver knew that."

"Oh, good," Martha said, and she sat down at the baby grand piano that in the sun was as shiny as patent leather.

Oliver and Esther took a back road to the cemetery. It was longer, more private. The day was gentle. They walked in a swinging rhythm. "We walk well together," Oliver said, but except for that they didn't talk. When they came to the edge of the village, beyond the last house, Esther stopped, posed, while a yellow warbler in a tree nearby sang his fluted song. "I can't bear it!" she said. "It's so beautiful!"

"Esther!" Oliver reached out to put his arm around her waist, but with a low laugh she twisted away and ran from him.

"Catch me! Catch me if you can!"

"You little devil!" he said when he came to where she had stopped to get her breath, her mouth half open with laughter, and he leaned forward to kiss her.

"The flowers!" she cried. "Watch out! They bruise if just a hard wind hits them!"

"To hell with *them*!" He threw the flowers down to have both arms free. "There!" he said after a time. "Are you bruised? Would you know that a hard wind had hit you?" He released her abruptly, an expression of astonishment on his face, but she rested against him unmoving, her head on his chest, bent a little, submissive. "Has anyone told you how beautiful you are when you've been running?" He stroked her hair as he might have stroked a child's.

"I guess we'd better salvage our bouquet," he said at last, and together they stooped and gathered the daffodils up from where they lay strewn on the earth, a confusion of pure yellow trumpets and translucent, watery-green stems.

"You haunt me," he said. "Your voice—it runs in my head. Since service this morning I haven't heard a sound but your voice. I don't have any other excuse or apology."

They walked on slowly. She didn't speak until they

reached the Henderson plot and had got fresh water and put the flowers in the deep metal container that stood on a standard before the granite shaft. "You don't need an excuse," she said then, trying to persuade the daffodils to stand more upright than they seemed inclined to. "No apology." Over the drooping flowers she looked at him somberly. "What are we going to do, Oliver?"

He didn't answer. They walked back along the country road by which they had come. "What did he mean to you, that other man?" Oliver asked.

"What man?"

"That fellow you ran off with."

"What on earth are you talking about?"

"Do you think I don't know about it?"

"Oliver, I was practically a *child*!"

"You were no child. What did he mean to you?"

Esther was silent. They passed the place where he had kissed her. "It was so long ago," she said.

He waited.

Finally she said, "Nothing. . . . Everything in the world. Don't you understand? I never had a chance to find out."

Oliver and Esther sang together the first Sunday in June—"How Beautiful upon the Mountain"—and from the way everyone spoke they must have raised gooseflesh on half the congregation. Martha didn't know a thing about their plans until choir rehearsal the Thursday before, when they stayed after the others had left and asked her to play the accompaniment for them. "We've been practicing it Sundays," Esther said in answer to Martha's surprise. She busied herself arranging the music on the piano rack, and when she had to look at Martha finally, it was with her eyebrows raised. "When you've been occupied."

"But Lucy . . ."

"I told you," Oliver said, "remember? It's too high for Lucy. She saw it herself after a while."

"*Heard* it, you mean." With a little laugh Esther corrected him.

Oliver reached over to rumple Esther's hair. "'Heard it' is good!"

"Oh, stop," Esther said. "You embarrass me." But she laughed again—that same light, teasing laugh.

It made Martha uncomfortable. "It's funny Lucy didn't say anything," she said.

"Probably didn't think it was worth mentioning," Oliver assured her.

Perhaps he was right. At any rate Lucy didn't seem to want to talk about it when Martha saw her the next day. "What made you give it up?" Martha asked.

"Nothing *made* me."

"But I thought Oliver got that arrangement especially for you."

"He did," Lucy said, "but he and Essie seemed to fancy themselves so, trying it over—oh, let's forget it, it's really not important. How was the Junior Department picnic?"

"Oh, Lucy, I think I've never had such a good time in my life! All laughing and the sun shining and buttercups and daisies thick as a carpet!" She shrugged at the impossibility of doing it justice.

"I've come to take you to lunch," David had said. He'd appeared at the side door that led into the den.

"Why, David!" she'd said.

"With the Junior Department!" He had roared with laughter. "We're going to pick buttercups and daisies for Children's Day, and it's ballooned into a picnic."

"But I've got cookies in the oven."

"What could be better?" he'd said. "I'll wait. We can take them with us."

"But how about Essie? She's down at Maybelle's having her hair done."

"'But . . . but . . . but. . . .' Leave her a note."

They'd laughed Essie off.

They ate beside the outlet, and the little girls were like birds darting through the field to pull the flowers from the earth and bring them to the spot David had made by the water, where the stems would keep wet—their chatter as sweet, Martha thought, dropping down to rest when there were more than enough and still no one wanted to leave. She sat beside the mound of white and waxy-yellow flowers, her weight back on her hands, her face tilted up—lightheaded from sun and happiness and the pungency of the daisy stems. From across the field she could hear David's voice through the chirruping of the children. David was bent over, intent on something, and the little girls were gathered around him, watching. Whatever they were saying had a secret sound.

Then they all came running, and they pushed that dirty, neglected Anderson child forward. "Close your eyes!" they called, and Martha heard them rustling closer. Something soft dropped down onto her head. "We've crowned you!" they shouted. "Queen of the daisies!" and they took hands and danced in a circle around her, madcap. A few steps away, David watched from the shade of a wild apple tree. The children ran off, shrieking like hoodlums. But the Anderson child ran back. "You really do look like a queen," she said shyly, and she stooped and stroked the sleeve of the pink cashmere sweater Martha was wearing. "Pretty," she said.

Martha caught the child to her, dirt and all. "Why, thank you, darling," she said, and over the child's head she saw David smiling down on her.

"The sweater or Miss Henderson, Dottie?" he asked.

"Miss Henderson," Dottie said, and she wriggled away and ran after the others.

"That's an intelligent child," David said. As he held out his hand and pulled her to her feet, Martha felt the warmth of her cheeks surge through her.

"Essie, what do you think of David?" Martha asked that night from behind the curtain of her hair. They were upstairs together in the marble-fixtured bathroom, doing their one hundred strokes. The bathroom, like the kitchen below, was large enough to hold a rocking chair, though this one was small, low; they had been rocked in it when they were babies.

Esther brushed a strand arm's length and examined it critically. "Oh, I don't know." She spoke with reservation. "Why, Marty?"

"I was just thinking what a fine person he is."

Esther considered. "Yes, I think I'd say that. Fine and very sincere—about his work, anyway."

"He can be wonderful fun, too," Martha said. She laughed. "You should have been along this afternoon."

"Well, if you remember, I hardly had a choice," Esther said in a brittle voice.

"Essie, you *did* care!" Martha shook her hair aside to look at Esther, but Esther was at the mirror, busy with water-wave combs, and Martha couldn't see her face.

"Don't be silly," Esther said. "Why should *I* care?"

But Martha knew she was hurt. Even so, she couldn't stop. "I wish Mama might have lived to know him better," she said.

"Whatever for? Mama knew him well enough. She felt about him the same way I do—she respected him, especially as a preacher. David's the kind of person you have to respect. It's just—"

"Just what?" Martha pursued it, though her heart was thumping unpleasantly.

"Just that he seems—well, uncouth, the way he goes about, and those big, calloused hands."

"I've always thought how strong his hands are," Martha said. She let the brush lie in her lap.

Immediately, Esther sounded sorry. "It's probably because I'm so much like Mama. We have more romance in us. We want a man to be—aesthetic, I guess that's what I'm trying to say. Really, it's nothing that matters if you're sure he's what you want."

"What I *want*! I was thinking of him as a friend— a friend of the family." With short, brisk strokes, Martha brushed her hair to the top of her head, where she tied it with a narrow velvet ribbon, tight.

"That's not the way he feels about you!"

"Why, Esther Henderson, whatever makes you say such a thing!"

Esther shrugged. "It's as plain as the nose on your face. You only want to hear me say it. Look how you're blushing!"

"That's sunburn," Martha protested.

But in the north bedroom they had been sharing for comfort since their mother's death, when she had kissed Esther good night and put out the light and opened the shutters and got into bed, Martha couldn't sleep. "Essie," she said some time later, "if it should be true, what you said—supposing—would you mind?"

There was no answer. Funny, Martha could have sworn that Esther hadn't gone to sleep, either.

Next morning, without a word's being said—as if some kind of agreement beyond words had been reached the night before—they moved back to their own rooms.

Two weeks after Esther and Oliver had sung together, Lucy and Oliver sang "This Is My Task" at the Sunday morning service. They'd been singing it at least once a year for as far back as anyone could remember. It wasn't music that called for feeling, but a good many people spoke of how nice it was to hear it again, and they fussed over Lucy in the vestibule afterward. Lucy had fussed over herself. She had a high-geared look, with a spot of rouge standing out on each cheek, and she'd been to the La Belle Beauty Salon and had Maybelle put a marcel in her hair. Martha couldn't remember her ever getting so fixed up just for church. Lucy held Oliver back from going down to the basement with the choir after the recessional. She kept him beside her, hanging onto his arms, her smile too bright and a brightness like an uncovered light bulb at the front of her eyes.

Madame Lovett rocked up to the two of them.

Madame Lovett was the great-great-granddaughter of one of the founders of Pliny Falls—a woman of means and such prestige that her social life reached all the way to New York City. She lived in a beautiful old cobblestone house at the end of the village. Pockmarks in the stones showed where attacks had been made in the old days, and in the stone barn to one side at the back there were slits just wide enough for a musket which had served to stand off the enemy who might be approaching up the bank from the river bed. She belonged to the most exclusive of the clubs—her mother had started it—and when she was in town was a faithful attendant at church, but the days of her life, like her house, lay at a remove from the life of the village. Who was there equipped to be an equal? Except Emmeline Henderson. Madame Lovett had been Emmeline Henderson's dear friend, an established guest at Christmas dinner in her home. When they were children, Martha and Esther wore little gold hearts on slender chains that she had brought them from Tiffany's, their initials entwined on the face in loops of engraving. They called her Aunt Laura.

"It's a message we can't hear too often," Madame Lovett said to Lucy and Oliver in her booming voice. "And I tell you it's refreshing to see a husband and wife who can share their pleasures as well as their *tasks*." She gave them an approving tap on their linked arms with the palm-leaf fan she carried from the first of June on.

David seemed gratified. He went home with the girls for dinner—a jovial guest. A weight she hadn't known she'd been carrying lifted from Martha.

4

*W*HOEVER would have believed that a summer so close to grief could turn to joy like this. Or pass so quickly. "Oh, stay a little longer"—it sounded a refrain to David's "Don't you think I should be going?" on the times when, driving by the house, he would drop in for a visit. It seemed as if he and Martha would never come to an end of what they had to tell each other.

One Thursday after choir rehearsal, Lucy and Oliver and David came with the girls back to the big house and they had tea and toast and cold roast chicken and pound cake Esther had made from their mother's recipe, with rose water for flavoring. When

THE WINE OF ASTONISHMENT

David had finished the last crumb, Esther said, "Come on, let's sing!"—looking to Oliver.

Oliver slanted his eyes at Lucy—a question—and after a second's hesitation Lucy said, "All right." Then she clapped her hands in an artificial way and said, "What a marvelous idea!" That's how Lucy was these days—an exaggeration of herself. Her long, thin, knobby hands were never still. Now she hopped up from the table and led the way to the drawing room, swishing her skirt, laughing high back over her shoulder. Martha sat down at the piano and the four of them stood behind her, around the bench. "Tell you what, David," Lucy said. "If you're game to try the bass, I'll try alto!" She held out her arms. "Soprano"—she drew Esther to her on the left. "Tenor"—and Oliver to her on the right. "Alto and bass! A quartet!"

With Martha coming down hard on the lower parts, they began with "Drink to Me Only." After the first time through, Oliver shifted away from Lucy. "Alto would be less competition for David," he explained, sidling around to Esther's left.

David said, "Suits me. Who wouldn't sing better with an arm around Lucy than around you!" and they circled each other again and put their heads close, and they sang and sang, ending with "Shall We

Gather at the River." Martha rolled the chords and syncopated the rhythm with extra beats in the bass. "We could be really good!" Oliver said when they were leaving, and they all said they must get together often, the five of them.

They did. Sometimes, with the little boys packed off to bed, they'd have a late supper at Lucy and Oliver's and sing through the evening. Other times, they took the children along and went off on picnics. One night, Hazel Pollock came to stay with the boys and they drove to Syracuse, where David treated them all to a movie.

And every morning Esther and Oliver ran into each other down street. They had worked out inconspicuous ways of meeting. The post office was one; they went for mail at the same time, just long enough after it had been put out for the first relay to have emptied their boxes and gone. Never together but meeting there casually and sauntering off for a few minutes' talk at the curb before Oliver gave her arm a little squeeze, murmured "Darling" in a strangled voice, and crossed the street to his insurance office while Esther went on to the grocery store, or home.

"Did you see anyone?" Martha asked invariably when Esther came back, and Esther never lied.

"Oh, Blanche and Rebecca Daniels," she might say. "And Oliver was in at the post office, picking up his mail." She spoke of him easily, as incidentally as before, though if he were near, color rose high in her cheeks.

"How did Oliver seem?" Martha asked one morning. "Lucy acted worried about him the other day when I was over there."

"Worried?" Esther carried an envelope to the wastebasket; her back was to Martha. "Did she say why?"

"Just that he'd been jumpy and irritable since spring. Not like himself. She didn't seem to know what could be wrong unless he was overworking. She wants to get him away."

"I didn't notice anything different," Esther said. "He didn't speak of it."

"If you ask me," Martha said, "Lucy's the one who needs to get away. She has an awfully funny look around the eyes."

August came so soon. Night after night the sun set red, round, hard—no hint of softening at the horizon. The heat was unrelieved. Except where Esther kept the hose going all day long, the earth around

the house hardened, the grass seared. Dirt from the
street dulled the larch to gray; when it stirred, the
branches gave off puffs of dust. The gladioli were
a disappointment. It took twice as many to make a
show at church, and afterward, at the cemetery, they
looked stunted in the metal flower holder there.

It was the month of vacations. David went off first,
his old Columbia touring car packed tight with a tent
and gear for a fishing trip in Canada. Martha knitted
him a pair of heavy, black-ribbed socks for a going-
away present. She and Esther had a dinner party for
him, and Martha bustled about until Esther called her
"Old Mother Hen" and took over herself.

Esther could be sweet. She put a wave in Martha's
hair. She hurried into her own clothes any which way
and came into Martha's room and said, "Here, sit
down," and combed her soft brown hair and pinned it
in the back in a loose double wing. And she brought
a yellow rose from the bush beside the kitchen door
and fastened it in Martha's hair, and she daubed her
with Chypre behind each ear and lightly over her
wrists, and she stood back and looked her up and
down and smiled. "There," she said. "You've never
looked prettier!"

And Martha, free to look for herself, saw that it

was true. "Why, Essie," she said. "Why, Essie!" They hugged each other, but carefully, so as not to get mussed.

"Martha, you should always wear a flower in your hair," David said. The others had left, Esther had gone up to bed, and they were sitting together on the heavy, tufted, velvet-covered sofa in the drawing room. He lifted his hand and touched the rose, and ran his fingers from it down to the softness under her chin.

Delight swirled from the spot. Eddies of delight caressed her. "If it pleases you," she said in a drowsy voice.

"It pleases me."

"Oh, David," Martha said, turning toward him.

He moved his hand to bring her face close. "Do you know how much I'm going to miss you?"

"Tell me," she said, but without saying anything he kissed her—a circle of light little kisses around the outline of her face, and on her eyelids, and on her mouth a kiss so light it was as if he had just brushed her lips with his. "I've been wanting to do that for a long time," he said.

"What made you wait?"

Instead of answering, he took her in his arms and cradled her head on his shoulder. "Martha, my darling girl," he said, bending to kiss her ear. Then he set her aside abruptly and stood. "I must be on my way." He looked distressed.

"But why?"

"These things get out of hand too easily. Before you know it, they've moved beyond control."

"Sin?" she said. "Thou shalt not commit happiness?"

"Not this happiness without its consecration— and remember I have to be off by six in the morning."

At the door David kissed her on the forehead, as if he were bestowing a blessing.

All that night Martha lay awake. Not even the birds were astir when she got up and, carrying her clothes so as not to disturb Esther, went down to the den to dress. In the kitchen she boiled eggs and made coffee and sandwiches; she filled a paper bag with fruit and cookies—food enough for two men and yet it didn't seem enough, being so much less than she wanted to do for him. As she worked, she made a melody of four notes. She hummed it over and over—monotonous—as outside the birds seemed all to come to life at once and the thin layer of light at the base of the sky spread upward in a widening arc. It was quite light when she stepped out the door of the den.

David was bent over the running board, settling the last suitcase behind the rack. Martha saw him and hurried. He looked up, incredulous. "What's the meaning of this?" he greeted her in a whisper.

She kept her voice as low as his. "I was too happy to sleep. I got up to see you off. I had to see you off." She smiled. "Are you happy?"

David glanced up and down the street. It was empty. He kissed her. She yielded everything against him, but he took only another of those quick, delicate kisses. "Happy," he whispered.

"I packed you a lunch." She added her gift of food to the heaped-up seat. "I was afraid you might not stop to eat."

"My dear," he said. He went to the front and cranked the motor and climbed over the running board in behind the wheel.

Martha came round to stand at his side. "I guess I don't want to let you go," she said, placing her hands on the shuddering door.

David leaned down and touched his cheek to them briefly. "You have such beautiful hands," he said.

"You'll write?"

"I'll write." Then he shifted into low and the car moved, sputtering, along the street away from her. "Good-by." She could only see it; the motor covered the sound of his voice. She waved.

Martha walked back to the house slowly. In the den, waiting for Esther to come downstairs, she sat for an hour, studying her hands.

Two days later, Oliver and Lucy left with the boys for her mother's place in Vermont. In Pliny Falls, Martha and Esther lived for the mail. From mail time on, the day was dead. If there was a letter from David, Martha knew it by heart after a second reading, though she would read it again and again, going for reassurance that he cared behind the reports of canoe trips taken, of fish caught and grilled on outdoor fires, of the heady fragrance of coffee boiling in pine woods. There wasn't a phrase in one of them that couldn't have been read aloud from the pulpit. David was not a writer of love letters. They all ended, "Yours in Christ, David."

One day, Essie came home with a package postmarked Brattleboro, "Fragile" stamped all over it. She opened it in front of Martha—a box in a box in a box. "That Oliver!" she said, excited, picking one box out of another, and all that there was when she got to the end was a narrow strip of paper. "Hello, darling." Before she thought, she had read it aloud.

"Esther!" Martha was horrified.

Esther blushed so heavily that even her nose turned pink. "Oh, it's just a joke," she said.

"Let me see!" Martha reached for it.

Esther crushed the paper in her hand. "There's nothing to see. It's a silly old joke, that's all—I tell you, it's nothing."

From then on, Esther carried her mail off and read it in secret, and she shut herself into her room to write the long letters she sent off care of General Delivery; she carried them inside her purse to the collection box outside the post office.

"You haven't heard from Oliver again, have you?" Martha asked at intervals, her voice anxious.

"No." Esther could look her straight in the eye and deny it.

"I don't understand! Whatever could he have been thinking of! Why, what would Lucy say!"

"Oh, stop accusing me!" Martha drove Esther wild. "Leave it alone! I haven't done anything!"

"I'm not accusing you," Martha said. "Why should I? But I don't think it was very nice."

It was a relief to be going away, themselves. Yet even through the two weeks at Fourth Lake in the Adirondacks, the mail was what they lived for. The inn, a quiet place where they had stayed a number of years with their mother, felt as haunted as the big house they had left, and all the other guests turned out to be very young or elderly. Mornings, they walked together over pine-padded trails; they sat on the veranda and rocked the afternoons away. Evenings, there were cards, and always letters to write; they often went early to bed. And while at the end they traded names and addresses with a show of caring, for what it really mattered they might as well have stayed at home. Except, of course, that it was something to say to the people who *had* stayed, "And we slept under blankets every night!"

5

I GUESS the trouble was, we took ourselves
along." Martha tried to explain it to Lucy
when she went over to deliver the little linen pillows
she and Esther had stuffed with balsam, and for the
boys birch-bark canoes and the gum they had pried
from spruce trees on their morning walks.

"Didn't we all!" Lucy said. She was brown from
the sun, but she looked as tense as when she had left.
And thin!

"Of course it was a good rest and change." Martha
thought she would never get over feeling uncomfortable with Lucy because of that package of boxes.
"But it's wonderful to be back!"

Sunday was like a reunion—the day before Labor
Day. Vigorous from his weeks of weather and life in

a tent, David preached on Christ's gathering for his disciples men who worked with their hands. And the choir sang "Work for the Night Is Coming." Everyone wore an air of renewal.

David came home with the girls for dinner. At first he demurred. They had only just got home—he could eat at the Busy Bee and drop by later. Esther was the one who urged him. Martha felt relieved. She couldn't stop herself from keeping an eye on Esther, though she tried not to let Esther catch her watching. At church, Esther had not for a second gone near Oliver. "Nice!" she'd called to him across the choir room in the basement, with a wave of her hand, but that was all—and her voice had sounded cool. As soon as her gown was put away, she went to stand beside Martha until she was ready, too, and they could go along upstairs together.

At home, after dinner, Esther insisted on doing the dishes by herself. "I feel like it!" she said. "You two run along and talk." She put her hands in the middle of their backs and pushed them out of the kitchen.

"But you'll come in when they're finished," Martha said. "Promise! We want you!" She turned to David. "Tell her that we want her."

"Of course we want you, Esther," David said. "How could you think differently?"

Esther walked along the cemetery road. *I can't, I
can't, I can't* was the rhythm she walked to now,
though what she couldn't was as undefined as the
need that had brought her out. It had taken her over
without warning when she'd hung her apron up on
the pantry door and was smoothing down her hair,
getting ready to go in with the others. *I can't*, she'd
thought, and she'd got her coat and let herself out the
kitchen door quietly and had crossed the lawn at an
angle that would keep her from sight of the drawing-
room windows. And still she thought, *I can't*—so it
couldn't have been the hour with David and Martha,
could it?

On the road to the cemetery, head down, she was
too deep in herself to hear Oliver come sprinting after her.

"Saw you from the back yard," Oliver said, stopping to catch his breath. "I've been watching for
you." He seized her arm and capered at her side like a
puppy. He held her arm close against him and he
pranced. "These last weeks without you have been
hell!"

Esther pulled her arm away. "I can't," she said.

Oliver's face lost its color and expression together.
"Can't what?" He spoke roughly.

"Not so long as there's Lucy!" She snatched her arm as though she had not already taken it from him. "Can't you see that I can't?" and she ran in through the cemetery gate and up the winding, rutted road, impervious to the faces of the Sunday visitors lifted, inquisitive, over their flowers where they tended their dead.

Beside the Henderson monument Esther flung herself to her knees and threw her arms around the shaft. The edges of granite bit into the soft undersurface of her arms. *How can I?*

"But where did you *go?*"

"Just for a walk." Esther's mood was cold. "Can't I go for a walk if I want to?"

"But *why?* I surely made it clear we wanted you to come in with us when the dishes were done. We expected you. I've been frantic, walking up and down, alone here, looking out windows, imagining—"

"I've already told you I'm sorry if you were silly enough to worry."

"'Silly!' There I was, calling, hunting the place over—and then having to pretend it was nothing— perfectly natural you should have chased off without even bothering to come say good-by or where you were going. I made excuses, but I don't know what David must have thought, his first Sunday back. He left almost right away. A guest in your own house!"

"Your guest," Esther said.

"Essie, how can you say such a thing! When you've told me time and again you didn't mind."

Esther's voice was dead level. The muscles around her lips tightened. "I *don't* mind. So far as I'm concerned, you can have David Rathbone here any time, all the time, if it gives you pleasure—I hope you will. But if I want to go for a walk while he's here without coming in and asking your permission, I'll go."

"You know it wasn't that." Rigid, they glared at one another. Then Esther moved toward the hall. In a few seconds Martha followed her. "Did you go alone?"

Esther hesitated. "And supposing I didn't?"

To help herself, Martha couldn't keep her voice from rising. "Essie, I don't understand you!"

Esther didn't speak.

"Did you go with Oliver?"

"Oh, leave me alone!" Esther shouted with so much passion that Martha stepped back.

"Essie, what's wrong?"

Instead of answering, Esther fled up the stairs. Above, a door slammed hard enough for the sound to carry dully down the carpet-deadened stairway.

"I've brought you up some tea and toast, Essie—it's almost nine. Aren't you hungry?" Martha stood by the bed. She held the tray with both hands.

Esther lay face down. She shook her head on the pillow, without turning over.

"Have I done something to hurt you?"

Esther shook her head again.

"You're sure?"

Esther's head moved up and down on the pillow, and after a minute more Martha carried the tray back to the kitchen.

"No, no," Esther said next morning as she sat, white and languid, over her coffee. "It has nothing to do with you. I'm telling you the truth."

Martha's heart raced. "Is it David?"

"It has nothing to do with David," Esther said in the same flat voice. "And I'm sorry if I embarrassed you in front of him."

"I'm over it—don't have it on your mind." Martha poured herself another cup of coffee. Adding cream and sugar, she stirred and stirred and stirred.

"Life seems so . . ." Esther began after a bit. She

64

spread her arms, then let them fall limply. "I guess I'm depressed."

Martha was clearing up the supper dishes when Esther came to the kitchen. "I'm going out, Marty," she said. "I think I'll feel better for some air."

Martha looked at her doubtfully. "Are you sure you're up to it? You scarcely touched your supper."

"I'm all right. I just wasn't hungry."

"Would you like company?"

"I think I'd rather go alone if you don't mind."

"As you like." The day before had left its mark.

"I won't be long," Esther called back from the door. "Don't worry." Out on the sidewalk, she paused. Up the road a piece, she told herself. Not the cemetery. But when she came to the entrance she could no more not turn in between the cobblestone posts, under the wrought-iron hoop than she could question the certainty that Oliver was there, waiting. She ran straight to him, and she threw herself against him, sobbing.

"Sh! Sh!" he soothed her. "Sh, love, my darling." They rocked back and forth. Oliver's face was haggard. "If you hadn't come soon!" he said. "I've been through hell! Hell! Never closed my eyes all night— today, driving through the country—I haven't been home—"

"Dearest," Esther said. She reached up to put her hand on his face. The bristles felt strange to her touch, and she left her hand there.

"It doesn't matter now," he said over her head. "Just that you're here. Nothing else."

"Not Lucy?"

"Nothing. That's been wrong from the start. Always."

"Not like this?"

"Nothing has ever been like this," he said, and, against him, she laughed a low laugh of satisfaction.

Then she pushed away and looked into his eyes. "Nothing *could* be like this if it wasn't right, could it, Oliver?"

His hands made a frame around her face. He looked back at her steadily. "The one thing on God's earth I know, my darling, is that feeling like this is stronger than what anyone thinks or says. It has to be right."

"What will you tell Lucy?"

Oliver reached in his pocket for a cigarette. His hands twitched as he lighted it. He stroked his mustache. "Why, I'll tell her that I love you—that we've found we love each other."

"And if she won't let you go?"

"Oh, Lucy will let me go quick enough once she

knows how it is with us. I'm pretty sure she suspects already. She'll probably take the boys and go to her mother's. I'll support them, of course. She'd be happier there. She's never liked it here as well as in Vermont."

"And the boys?"

"They'll be all right. Better off. It's no good for kids to grow up in a home that's not happy."

"But what if she won't?"

"You don't need to trouble yourself about *that*. Lucy's all common sense. She'll see it our way. I know her inside out." Arm in arm they started down the road toward the gate. "No poetry," he said. That's been the trouble between us. She's never understood me, not really—she hasn't any poetry."

"We'll have children," Esther said in a dreamy voice. "It isn't too late. I want to give you a child, Oliver."

Oliver's arm in hers tightened.

Back at the house, Esther caught hold of Martha and whirled her in a circle. "I'm starved!" she cried. "Come on out to the kitchen!" She shone.

"Well!" Martha said, relieved. "You look like a different person. Fresh air must have been just what you needed."

When Esther and Oliver began to practice duets together regularly, there wasn't a thing Martha could do about it. She tried. "I don't care if it *is* only a song," she said. "Lucy will be hurt."

"What of it?" Esther's self-possession never cracked these days.

"What *of* it!"

"Lucy gives me a pain. Balanced meals. Budgets. The program for Women's League. What's going on in the world. That's all she cares about. What does *she* know about poetry? Why, she no more understands Oliver than the man in the moon."

Martha looked puzzled. "Does Oliver write poetry?"

"*Write poetry!* That's just what I'm talking about! Oliver's the first person in my whole life who's understood me. And you might as well know sooner as later what he means to me."

Martha sat down so hard her spine felt jarred its full length. "That package this summer," she began. "I *knew* . . ." She stared up at Esther.

Esther's eyes blazed straight back. "Oliver and I love each other, if that's what you're hinting at." She stood tall. Stretched up. "He and Lucy—why, that marriage has been a mistake from the start." She dismissed it with a gesture.

"Essie, how can you talk like that!"

"I'm only saying what Oliver said."

"Oliver Bradley said that to you about *Lucy*?"

"He did."

"Essie . . ." Martha paused. "Essie, you don't know what you're doing. Oliver Bradley is a married man. With *children*. It isn't *right*."

Esther smiled. All of a sudden she looked perfectly serene. "It's the rightest thing that's ever happened to me," she said.

"I tell you it isn't. It's a terrible thing to come between a husband and wife."

"Well, since Oliver feels exactly the same way I do, I'm hardly coming *between* anybody, am I?"

"It's wrong, Esther Henderson, and you know it. The Bible—"

"Don't think you can go quoting the Bible at me just because you're in love with the minister, Marty."

"Essie!"

"But if quoting's what you want, how about '. . . and the greatest of these is love'?"

"I warn you, people will *talk*."

"Let them." Esther was still smiling.

Martha started to cry.

"I'm sorry you feel like this," Esther said out of her serenity, "but that's the way it is. I'm going upstairs now. I don't want to say another word about it."

"Lucy Bradley is my best friend," Martha kept saying, but she was crying so hard nobody could have made it out.

"Well, I've told Martha," Esther announced to Oliver outside the post office next morning.

"You've *what?*" Oliver grabbed her arm so hard it was like a shake. "*What* did you tell her?"

"Just that we love each other. That you and Lucy never had."

"You told Martha *that?*"

"I had to. I had to get things clear. She was after me about the duets."

"My God." Oliver reached up to his breast pocket for the handkerchief he always wore folded in a trim arrangement of triangles. He took it out carefully, keeping its shape. "What did she say?"

"She told me I didn't know what I was doing. Then she cried."

"Oh, Christ," Oliver said.

"What did Lucy say?"

"Lucy?"

"Oliver, do you mean to tell me that you haven't *told* Lucy?"

Oliver patted his face with his folded handkerchief. "Well, I haven't come out in so many words"—he looked sheepish—"but I'm working on it."

Esther bent away from him. "'Working on it!'" she said. "'Working!'" She had to turn aside to smile a false, bright smile as Mrs. Hiram Sims went by. "What work is there but to come out and *tell* her!"

"Sh!" Oliver cautioned, and he leaned toward her; the distance between them never changed. "Now don't go getting excited. A break like this has to be led up to. . . . The timing has to be right. You don't understand." He ran the corner of the folded handkerchief along the dapper line of his mustache, one side and then the other.

"I understand this much!" Esther began, when Oliver laid a hand on her arm.

"Now don't get mad," he said. "If you get mad at me, too, I can't go on. I'm serious."

There were tears in his eyes. Esther saw them, appalled. They washed every trace of easy confidence away. His face showed worn and distraught. "Oliver!" she said.

"I've got to do it my own way! I've got to have time!" His eyes were pale with tears; they begged. "Won't you give me time? Just a little time?"

Esther's anger dissolved. "It isn't that," she said, her voice low. "It's just—if you've changed your mind, you should tell me now, before . . . Not let me go on like this."

For a moment they stood without speaking, each swaying in, unaware, toward the other. "Darling!" Oliver muttered. "As God is my witness!" before, with a nod, he turned away. Walking unevenly, he crossed Main Street to his office next to the dust-filmed window of the Cayuga County Bank and Trust.

"About those duets," Oliver said to Esther a few days later. "Maybe we ought to let them wait for a while. No use setting everyone on their tin ear about us."

"And *who's* on their tin ear?"

"Well, you said the other day that Martha—"

"I took care of Martha," Esther said. "Who else, pray?"

"You know how it is." Oliver's eyes met hers and slid away. "Lucy and I have always sung them together. Naturally, she expects it—she—"

"'Naturally!' *Tell* her! I guess if I could tell my own sister!"

"Lucy isn't my sister." Oliver still didn't look at her; his eyes flitted about. "God knows I've tried. She doesn't give me an opening. She takes it for granted—you can't do much when a person . . . David's asked her if we'd sing two weeks from Sunday. She spends half her time practicing. I can't get out of it."

"Say you won't. Make a scene."

"She'd only laugh. If you knew what it was like— meaning something with your whole heart, to have her laugh!"

"Why," Esther said, "I had no idea Lucy was so— why, I don't see how anyone could *be* so insensitive."

"You wouldn't," Oliver said in a tender voice. "All sensitivity the way you are." His shoulders twitched. "God," he said. "I can't take much more of it. Those duets aren't worth it."

"They're worth it to me," Esther said. "I tell you right now they're worth it to me."

6

ALMOST every Sunday afternoon Martha and David sat together in the drawing room on the tufted velvet sofa, talking. For Martha, Sunday afternoon was the cherished point by which time was marked in its passing. The closeness, though David maintained whatever bounds of control he had set for himself: holding her hand affectionately as they talked; throwing an arm over her shoulder and drawing her toward him to rest her head on his shoulder; a light kiss in the hall when he was leaving. It will come, she thought, counting on the happiness she sensed in him when he was near her. Often Esther joined them around six for hot chocolate and toast. The three of them could live happily together—Martha was certain of it.

"I don't know what I'd do without you, Martha," David said at the end of an afternoon they'd spent together planning the program for Harvest Sunday.

"Look out you don't confuse me with an assistant minister!" she said, laughing, mindful of Lucy's warning.

"I would never do that," he said. "That isn't how I feel about you at all."

"I wish sometime you'd tell me."

"You can be sure that I will," he said, but it was already November and he hadn't spoken a word of love or of loving.

"Let's have Lucy and Oliver and Teddy and Bud for Thanksgiving this year," Martha said to Esther one morning. "And David, of course."

"Of course," Esther said.

If the tone was sardonic, Martha didn't acknowledge it. "After service. It would mean eating early—that service is over by noon—but we could manage. And then before the boys had to get home for their naps we could all go for a walk in the country."

"Or make a snow man if the snow holds. It's just right," Esther said. "Remember the fun we used to have, and Mr. Daniels helping at the end and bringing over an old hat and one of his pipes to finish him off in style?"

"Maybe we should invite the Danielses, too! They won't mind if the boys get excited and start running in circles."

The snow did hold, and after Thanksgiving dinner they got into galoshes and wool caps and mittens and went out front to work on the snow man. "With *this* manpower, we should make two," David said. "One to stand each side of the front steps." They chose up teams—Lucy and Martha and David and Teddy, and Esther and Oliver and Mr. Daniels and Bud. Rebecca said she would go fetch the hats and pipes and come back in a while and watch from inside.

"We need coal for their eyes," Oliver said when the four balls were rolled and the two smaller were set in place on the larger. "I'll run into the house and get it."

"The anthracite in the cellar is what you want," Esther said. "I'll show you."

They were gone so long that Lucy finally sent Teddy in to find them. "Oh, we were just being fussy to get pieces that matched," Esther said airily when they came out.

"Martha, have you wondered if things are all right between Lucy and Oliver?" David asked the next Sunday, as he was leaving.

"What makes you ask?"

"Lucy looks strained and unhappy to me. She has all fall, and I noticed it particularly on Thanksgiving. Not at all herself. I felt concerned."

"I feel concerned, too," was as much as Martha could bring herself to say.

"You don't know what the trouble might be, do you? Has she spoken to you about it?"

Martha shook her head. At least it was a true answer to his second question.

"There's some talk."

"Oh?"

"Probably nothing in it—there usually isn't. 'Thou shalt not gossip' ought to have been an eleventh commandment. But if there should be, Martha, I must tell you that I could not condone it. The deliberate breaking up of a home is sacrilege." He was putting on his coat and his back was to her. When he said goodnight, he held her to him a moment, and without kissing her he laid his cheek against hers. Martha sensed regret in the act—or was it her regret, knowing the truth and having withheld it from him?

Later that week, Rebecca Daniels stopped by.

"Yoo-hoo!" she called at the back door, and when Martha answered over the wail of the Hoover she was using in the upstairs hall, Rebecca lumbered her way to the landing and sank onto the seat under the stained-glass window. "Just saw Esther off on her assignation," she said when Martha had come down the four steps to join her. "Thought this was as good a time as any." She was wheezing from the stairs.

"Her what?"

Rebecca lowered her voice. "I won't say they don't sound good," she confided.

"I don't know what on earth you're talking about," Martha said. But she did. She'd known the second Rebecca spoke Esther's name.

Rebecca went right on. "If you ask me, they sound *too* good, singing their songs like a pair of orioles calling to each other in mating season—first one, then the other, then the two of them together." She waved her hands in a conducting motion. "And you can say what you like, Martha, choir or no choir, a man's place is by the side of his wife. I'm not the only one who feels it or I'd never have come. This isn't easy for me, don't think it is—your own sister, and the regard I always held for your ma. But I said to Henry, and I say it to you, 'Better me than perhaps someone they aren't so close to.'"

"Are you talking about Esther's *singing*?" Martha got in when Rebecca paused for breath. The tone of her voice kept a space between them.

"There!" Rebecca said. "It *is* like I said to Henry. 'It may be she don't even know. It's a strange thing,' I said, 'how the nearest affected are always last to find out.'" She squinted in scrutiny, but Martha held her face closed. So Rebecca came right out with it. "They meet," she said. "Oh, they pretend—'Hel*lo*!' they say"—she made her voice affected, throaty, to sound like Esther; Martha cringed to recognize it. "Playing they're surprised. As if everybody in town wasn't on to them, mooning at the curb the length of Main Street, off to the cemetery, though now it's getting colder I don't know where they'll take to. Oh, they've been seen! Carrying on!"

Martha stiffened. "Like a ramrod," Mrs. Daniels reported to Mr. Daniels that evening, "Hoity-toity, letting on she didn't beleive a word. I can tell you I pulled in my horns quick enough. I put it off onto the church. 'I only mention it because I don't like to see trouble brewing in the church,' I said. 'There's nothing sorer nor longer to heal, as you'd know if you'd been through that *to* do the Baptists had over their minister before you could remember. So I just thought if I said a word to you, Martha, you might be able to do something about it before people get to talking more than they are already.'"

"But land," she said the morning after, over the back fence to Mrs. Beers. "I don't expect anything to come of it. Not now. She didn't pull the wool over *my* eyes. Martha knows, right enough. She gave it away: she never asked me a question."

"Didn't need to," Mrs. Beers agreed.

"That old biddy!" Esther flared when Martha told her, standing taut, half sick with shame, in the middle of the kitchen, where she'd waited, not doing a thing, since Mrs. Daniels left. "Her mouth's as loose as ashes!"

"But Essie, at least discuss it."

"There's nothing to discuss," Esther said, and she flounced off up to her room.

Martha stood quite still while the steam in the kettle rose higher and higher. Almost blindly she reached for the strainer that lay on the drainboard by the sink. As hard as she could, she hurled it onto the floor at her feet. It bounced once before it skidded on the waxed linoleum all the way across the kitchen floor.

––––––––

Martha couldn't bear to look Lucy in the face any more, though they didn't acknowledge that things were different between them. They just no longer went back and forth the way they had. Martha wondered if Lucy knew. If she knew what? What was there to know? Night after night, Martha walked her bedroom floor, wringing her hands for relief from wondering. No learning from Esther. Esther stayed as secret as a clam. You couldn't reach her, not to question or appeal to or to criticize. She was pleasant enough—the shell of her, that is. They talked. They talked over plans for Christmas.

Esther had an idea. She came down to breakfast with it one morning, all smiles. "Let's have our pictures taken for Christmas," she said. "Good ones. We could go to Lewisohn's in Syracuse. We haven't had pictures since we were little—I mean pictures that did anything more than look like us. I'm going to call this minute for an appointment!"

Her enthusiasm was infectious. Martha laughed. "You'd better wait till they open," she said. "It isn't eight-thirty."

"I'd love to have a nice picture of you, Marty," Esther said. "You've really looked handsome all fall. I'll fix your hair, and we can try on clothes to see what looks best around the neck. Though I'm pretty sure that what I want is a velvet drape."

"I could give one to David," Martha said. "I've been wondering what on earth to give him."

"Good idea," Esther said.

The pictures were a triumph. Deciding among the proofs took days, they all came out so well, though Esther complained that Martha's had a sad look about the mouth. "You'll have to watch it!" she said. "You'll get lines!" They ordered six pictures apiece, in the medium size, the most expensive finish. Martha's were for David, for Esther, for Lucy, for herself (the keeping of a record) and two to have on hand. Esther didn't say about hers. They had them mailed separately. Esther brought the packages from the post office, lilting with good spirits; she sneaked hers upstairs without letting Martha have a look. "Christmas!" she cried when Martha asked. "How can it be a surprise if you see it ahead?"

They were going to have Christmas dinner at home. They would take their baskets and packages around in the morning, but they would come back to the house, with dinner the way they'd always had it—Sid and Hortense Corbett from the factory, and Madame Lovett, and this year David for the sixth. It had come as a relief when Lucy made it definite that they would not spend any part of the day together.

"We're too much at sixes and sevens," she explained. She had brought over a quart of the venison mincemeat her mother sent every year from Vermont. "Bud's still edgy from the whooping cough, and you know how Christmas is anyway, with two kids underfoot. They're more than likely sick before the day even gets here, what with Santa Claus at Sunday School and not getting their sleep, and all that truck they stuff into themselves—and being half crazy over their presents. We're giving Bud a trike, by the way—one of those big-wheeled ones."

"That's wonderful," Martha said. "He'll love it."

"Oh, he'll love it all right, but it wasn't my idea. Oliver insisted. We can't afford it and he'd be as satisfied with a coaster wagon. We had quite an argument over it. Teddy's big present is roller skates. And a blackboard. He likes to draw pictures." She hesitated. She ran her hands through her hair. Her hair needed washing, and the marks of her fingers showed in the parts they left. "You've probably noticed Oliver isn't himself this fall." Her eyes met Martha's, but with reserve drawn over them; her face asked not to be questioned.

"Oh?"

"Nerves," Lucy said. "Oliver's quite a nervous person really, though you might not know it with all his fooling and joking. He has a nervous stomach. The least little thing upsets him. He works so hard—he has to keep on the go—and the insurance business hasn't been too good lately. He's feeling kind of unsettled. That's why I think it's good for him to be interested in his singing—it takes his mind off himself. I've been encouraging it." Her expression changed. Distress rose to the surface to show; it showed deeper than the two deep lines between her straight, fine brows. "Oh, well." She sighed. "Married people go through these times. You have to weather them. The only thing, I've decided, is just to go along and ignore it the best way I can. He'll get over it."

Her speaking cleared the air. Martha's eyes filled with tears, she was so grateful. "Wait a minute," she said, and she went out to the pantry and put sand tarts into a brown paper bag. "Tell the boys their Aunt Martha sent them," she said, and when Lucy left, she kissed her. "I wish you didn't look so tired. I wish there was something I could do. . . ."

7

*A*LL THE Christmas preparations were finished the night before, even to having the table set. They had to be; there wouldn't be time in the morning. Baskets to go to the families and old people Emmeline Henderson had always remembered at Christmas sat in a row in the hall, filled with things to eat: hams and cheeses and fruitcakes and preserves; in each, wrapped in holly paper, a box of homemade candy that Martha and Esther had a reputation for—fondant, peanut brittle, little hard red anise drops, seafoam. More personal packages spilled over the console table, with the mirror above it making them seem twice as many as they were. For hers, Esther had used blue paper, silver cord.

She'd done the tree in blue and silver, too. Long-needled pine. It brushed the ceiling in the drawing room. Sid Corbett had sent two of the men from the factory out to cut it for them; it had been his Christmas present to the family as long as they could remember, and the men who brought it in a factory truck always stayed to set it up and afterward have coffee and fried cakes out in the kitchen. This year, blue balls hung from top to bottom, and the bulbs on the strings of lights were all blue—iridescent; the only contrast was the strips of silver, ice-bright, lining every branch.

Martha missed the old ornaments—the plump birds and the thin, elongated angels, both feathered, the fat tinsel strung round and around, and the gaudy paper shapes and loops that she and Esther had made as children and their mother had kept over the years. But Esther was right; they *had* grown faded and shabby, and no doubt it was best to have things different this first Christmas alone. They didn't so much as open the Christmas-tree box. And this blue and silver tree was beautiful. Cold—according to your taste—but beautiful. Everyone who saw it spoke of how artistic Esther was. "Exotic," Esther called it. "I love things to be exotic!" she said when company complimented her, and Christmas Day she looked it, in a new blue silk dress the shade of the Christmas-tree balls, and a wide silver band around her hair.

Oliver couldn't stop talking about the way she looked. They had saved their call on the Bradleys for last. "We can only stay a minute, mind!" Martha was careful to say in the entryway. "We can't leave our turkey alone *too* long, he might get lonesome." She smiled at the little boys hanging onto her legs. But of course she and Esther had to take off their coats and boots and go in. Esther pirouetted in the middle of the living room, to show off her new dress.

"She's a Christmas angel!" Oliver exclaimed. "Angel, come down off that tree!"

"Oliver, for heaven's sake!" Lucy said, and she took Martha over to admire the new tricycle and blackboard.

Oliver ran his finger along the band on Esther's hair. He held the drapery of her skirt to one side, the better to admire her dress. "Gol*lee*! he said, and he whistled. "You look good enough to eat. Doesn't she?"

No one paid any attention.

"I ask you, *doesn't* she look good enough to eat?"

Lucy glanced at him. "I guess it would depend on how strong your stomach was," she said.

They laughed, but uneasily. Oliver's face colored the red-blond shade of his hair. He went over to lift Bud up and demonstrate the tricycle, and Martha reached hurriedly into the basket to pass out the presents they had brought: a bright-red top and a small cart of blocks for Bud, an erector set and a box of chalk for Teddy, sweaters for both boys, with mittens to match; they had a pretty slip for Lucy—Martha had shopped for it—and a tie for Oliver they had chosen together.

"Wow!" Oliver said, holding the tie out. "I'll be Old Man Brummel himself!" He gave Martha a kiss.

Teddy had opened the box of chalk. "Now what did you have to go and bring me chalk for when I've got all the chalk in the world!" he said, pointing to the broken sticks of white chalk lying on the blackboard shelf.

"Teddy!" Lucy said.

"No, no, it's Christmas," Martha said. "Goodness, I see that you have. I guess Santa forgot to tell me. But maybe you can use this, too. It's colored. You can make pictures with it. See? It's yellow and pink and orange."

Teddy trotted over the blackboard. Bud had scrambled off his tricycle and was busy with the new blocks.

"And now!" Martha said.

Esther crossed to the basket. "Let me!" she said, and she stooped and picked up the large flat package that had been put in first, so as not to bend the edges. "Wait till you see! 'To Lucy from Marty,'" she read from the card. "'With love.'" She handed Martha's picture to Lucy, and then she stooped again and took up another package, like the first except for being wrapped in blue and silver. "To Oliver from Esther," she announced. "No card!" She passed it to him with a flourish.

"What?" Oliver said. "No love?"

"'No card' is what I said."

"No love, no fair!" Oliver said.

"Marty!" Lucy cried. "How lovely." She looked from the picture to Martha and back to the picture again.

"Quick! Open yours!" Esther said to Oliver.

Oliver held the package flat against his side. "Not until you say 'With love.'"

"Oh, all right." Esther pretended to pout. "With love, since you insist."

"I insist." He tore off the wrapping.

"You couldn't have given me anything I'd think more of," Lucy said to Martha. "Look, Oliver."

But Oliver was looking at the photograph of Esther. "My God! Excuse me," he apologized at once. "It's just that I'm knocked off my pins. Why, this is the most beautiful thing I've ever seen in my life!"

"Do you really like it?" Esther went over to stand at his side. She examined the picture as if she'd never seen it before.

"Why, it's exquisite!" Oliver said. "It's—it's— why, it's Art, that's what it is. It's Art!"

"That's how I felt about it," Esther said. "I was pretty sure you'd like it. As a matter of fact, I had that pose finished up just for you. Marty didn't even know—did you, Marty? She'd only seen it in the proof. She thought it was too theatrical, but *I* like it."

They stood there studying it so long that Lucy and Martha joined them.

"It feels like me," Esther announced.

"Hm," Lucy said.

Still Martha didn't speak. Her heart had started that awful hammering against her throat, like the day in the kitchen after Rebecca Daniels's visit. It made her feel half sick—and on Christmas!

"I must say I agree with Martha, though," Lucy

said at last. "It's a wonderful job, but it's too arty for me, with all that velvet chucked under your chin and your eyes rolled up—looks as if you might be hunting for a vision. I like this one." She patted the photograph of Martha. "It's more natural. We'll keep them upstairs for company, and thank you both very much."

"We aren't going to keep *this* piece of art upstairs!" Oliver said. "We're going to keep it"—he glanced around the room—"right here on the piano. That's where *this* belongs." He lifted off the poinsettia, and one by one the piles of music; he swept off the tapestry that Lucy had draped over the top of the baby grand for protection. Exactly in the center of the shiny black surface, he stood Esther's picture.

Lucy went over and folded it together. "Art or no art," she said in what sounded like a perfectly casual voice, "there aren't going to be any photographs on *my* piano." She spread out the tapestry, her hands quick and precise. Her cheeks getting redder and redder, she piled the music back as it had been, and she brought the poinsettia from the bookcase, where Oliver had put it, and set it down with a thump.

"Essie! How could you!" Martha said as soon as the Bradley's door had closed behind them.

"How could I what?"

"Do what you just did." Martha felt dizzy with anger. "How *could* you!" She said it over and over.

But with Madame Lovett and David and the Corbetts coming for dinner, they managed. They made careful conversation that included each other. They put on a show of everything's being smooth between them until time came for the salad to be cleared and the hot mince pie with brandy sauce brought in. "Better let me," Martha suggested. "Remember, the last time you took it out too soon!"

Esther was already on her feet. "Stop criticizing me!" she shouted at Martha—in front of guests! "I made that pie and I'll decide when it's warm enough to serve!" and she rushed from the dining room.

Martha saw Hortense Corbett look across the table at her husband in a knowing way. She took a deep breath. "She's right." She looked straight at Hortense. "I *have* been criticizing her. I've been acting bossy and horrid. And if there's anything worse than being criticized when you've done nothing to deserve it, I don't know what it is." She said it firmly, and when, after a long wait, Esther came back into the room, Martha held out her hand. "Essie dear, I'm sorry," she said. "Forgive me."

"Oh, that's all right." Martha could see she'd been

crying. "I guess it must be too much Christmas. *I'm* sorry I lost my temper."

Madame Lovett came to the rescue. "Tempers are the Devil's Advocate!" she roared at them. Her voice was deep, louder every year as her hearing failed. "You have to wrestle them to the end, Esther, and don't you forget it. Right to the end. Why, the other day I got so mad over not being able to take myself off to the post office what with all the ice there was underfoot I threw my cane—an old woman like me! And then I couldn't so much as raise my hulk out of the chair. Had to wait for Gertie to come fetch it for me. Served me right. Mad at the universe, I guess." She cut into her pie. "Felt better for it, just the same," she concluded, and her shrewd eyes rested on each of them briefly.

Oh, Madame Lovett was a blessing. When it was time to leave, bundled into her velvet carriage boots and her ankle-length cape of fisher, the plume that circled her toque aflutter, secured by her corset, her cane, and David's right arm—after she'd made her thank-yous and good-bys, she'd taken her arm from David to pat Martha on the back. "Bear and forbear!" she'd roared. "That's what it takes. Bear and for-bear!" At the door she swung back. "And the more of the one, the more of t'other."

And somehow the anger had gone. When Martha found Esther up in her room that evening, sobbing in spasms that shook the bedframe, she took her in her arms and rocked her as if she were a child. Esther clung to her. Her tears soaked into the collar of Martha's dress halfway around the neck. They didn't say a word.

The hardest thing for Martha was that David didn't come back. With the dishes done and the tidying, and the extra table leaves replaced in their frame, with Esther asleep upstairs, she sat in the drawing room by the cannel-coal fire, in the eerie light of the blue bulbs on the Christmas tree, listening for him. When finally she put out the lights and opened the front door wide for a minute onto the frosted world beyond the pillars, she saw his car parked across the street, in front of Lucy and Oliver's.

Perhaps it was as well he didn't come that night. Out of worry and loneliness she might have turned Esther over to him in words. And Martha knew what he would say—he had already said it—and his chin would jut forward, his eyes alert against her. "This is a moral universe we live in!" Sin and its wages. Judgment. Yield not to temptation. The stuff of his sermons. Her sister. For a disloyal moment, Martha longed for old Dr. Westcott. Mellowed by his years of experience with frailty, Dr. Westcott would have taken Esther not for what they wished she might be but for what she was, and with loving kindness would have tried to lead her into something better. For her own happiness he would have done it. He would never have turned on her a disapproval with the weight of a whole moral universe behind it. But then, a good many members of the congregation complained that Dr. Wescott had become too easy-going as he grew old.

In her mind, Martha tried to make David understand. "It's her temperament, David. Headstrong—she has to be right! And it's no use scolding. Scolding only makes her more defiant. She suffers! Don't think she doesn't." But she would never be able to say it aloud; she could never let him hurt her with the answer she knew he would make.

Martha rested her weight on the banister as she climbed the stairs. In her right hand she carried the little box that held the locket David had given her for Christmas. He had dropped by with it Christmas Eve—his mother's locket, a silver oval outlined in tiny silver forget-me-nots, the chain a flat line of the tiny silver flowers. The locket was soft from time and wearing, and it opened on the faded picture of a staring, belligerent baby, his cheeks so distended he looked as though he had the mumps, and yet, even so, recognizable as David. When she saw it, Martha had laughed until she almost choked.

David had laughed with her. "If you want to see a face that only a mother could love!" He'd been the one to open the locket.

"Oh, I don't know that I'd agree to that!" Martha had said, but she couldn't stop laughing. "It's only because it looks so much like you," she explained.

David had become serious. "I want you to keep it for a talisman," he'd said, and he'd put his hands over hers. "Mother left so little, except what she was—as far back as I can remember, she wore this whenever she dressed up. My father gave it to her when I was born. I know it isn't valuable, but it's about the dearest thing I own."

"It will be to me," Martha promised. "As long as I live, I'll treasure it."

"It hurts to think how little she had," David said.

"That's isn't true. She had everything. She had you," Martha said, surprised at herself.

"Dear Martha!" David had said, and he had hugged her hard and kissed her with more urgency than he ever had before. "That's for Christmas."

Now, up in her room, Martha lifted the locket from its box. For a long time, standing quiet, she held it, her fingers closed over loosely while the silver took on the warmth of her hand and grew larger in that warmth. Then without opening the locket, without trying it on, she put it into the box, and she put the box in the back of her top right-hand dresser drawer, and she reached up to unfasten the sprig of holly she had pinned—for him—in her hair.

"You can say what you like about David," Martha burst out at Esther the morning after Christmas when they were making the beds. "At least he practices what he preaches!"

Across the hair mattress they had just turned, Esther looked at her, puzzled. "Why, Marty, I didn't say anything about David. I wasn't even thinking of him."

Martha was embarrassed. "Oh, you know what I mean!" she said vaguely.

Esther tossed the bottom sheet across the bed. "Practices what?" she asked.

Martha made a careful square corner. "Nothing," she said. "I don't know what I was thinking of."

Esther watched her, her eyes speculative. "Don't you?"

Sometimes Martha had the feeling that Esther could read what lay in her mind.

Everyone knew about the picture Esther had given to Oliver. Once Rebecca Daniels dropped over at the Bradley's just before supper the day after Christmas, it didn't take any time at all for word to get round. She was bringing gingerbread men, still warm from the oven, for the children, and as she opened the front door Oliver rushed toward her down the stairs. What with the tricycle out in the middle of the small square hall and the cartful of blocks tipped over flat, there was barely space for Rebecca, let alone the two of them. Oliver backed up two steps to let her by. He had the photograph under his arm. Rebecca stopped to peer at it. "Oh!" she cried. "A Christmas picture of the kiddies!"

"Bold as brass!" She could hardly wait to get home to report. "'A Christmas picture, all right, Aunt Rebecca,' he says, 'only not of the boys, not this year—couldn't afford it,' and with that he opened it up and pushed it under my nose. And *who* do you think it was, pushed into my face?"

"Well now, let me see." Deliberately, Henry Daniels took his pipe out of his mouth.

"Esther Henderson!"

"No!"

"Esther Henderson—the nerve of her. The nerve

of the two of them! Decked out in one of them velvet curtains and her eyes turned back in her head, looking like a houri. 'Good grief, Oliver!' I said. 'What's this doing *here?*'"

"You shouldn't have, Becky."

"Well, I did. It came right out of me."

"And did he give you an answer?"

"He did. 'Oh,' he says, slick as hair oil, 'it belongs on the piany. I was just bringing it down. For some reason, Teddy keeps carrying it off upstairs.'"

"Teddy!" Mr. Daniels looked confused. "Now why would Teddy do a thing like that?"

Mrs. Daniels laughed one short hoot. "Oh, Henry!" She shook her head over his innocence. "Don't be so easy. He never did, and it's a sign of the man, willing to put a thing like that off onto an innocent child. But Lucy was bellering at me to come out to the kitchen, so I didn't have the chance to pursue it. Not that there was any call to, not as it turned out. I didn't stop a minute and when I came along, Lucy came with me. She made a beeline for the setting-room arch, and if it wasn't to check up on her piany I haven't got eyes in *this* head. So I just took a good look for myself, and sure enough, there set Miss Esther square in the middle, big as life and twice as unnatural, and across the room Oliver Bradley folded away behind his paper, letting on he didn't even take in we was there."

Mr. Daniels shook his head.

"Lucy darkened over, but I didn't wait. A storm like that's best broken in the bosom."

Mr. Daniels picked up his pipe. It had gone out, and he examined it. "Ah," he said, "I don't like it, Becky. A nice young couple like that, with kiddies."

Mrs. Daniels left him, to hang up her coat and go along to the kitchen. She had supper on the oilcloth-covered table before she spoke again. "Henry," she began as they sat down, "I can't get out of my mind it's not Christian to set by and watch a fine home broke up and never lift a finger to prevent it. I did what *I* could, going to Martha that time, and all the further I got was just to jell her against me. You better say the blessing before everything's cold."

"For what we are about to receive dear Heavenly Father make us truly grateful Amen," Henry mumbled fast.

Rebecca served and passed him a sauce dish of creamed corn. "And what I've concluded is, as an elder of the church it's up to you to take steps."

"Ah, now, Becky, you know how I feel about interfering." Mr. Daniels tucked his napkin under his belt. "It's hard enough for a man to come on the answers for himself without undertaking to hunt them down for his neighbors. I don't like it, I said I didn't—especially not with the kiddies—but I wager it's more likely to blow by and nothing come of it if everybody keeps hands off than if they don't." He took a mouthful of stew and chewed it slowly. He swallowed. He wiped his mouth with his napkin. "Oliver Bradley's a good enough fellow in his way," he said then. "Good-natured, kind of easygoing. It's my guess he's been living with too much clutter and too little money for the bills, and not enough that's pretty to suit him. And there's Esther right across the street— no clutter, plenty of money, and artier than this town's got the time to appreciate. Why, comparison to what *he* has, she'd look like a bed of roses. But leave it a while, he'll find she's full of prickers as our old Dorothy Perkins out by the barn, and Lucy's been his woman all along." He took another forkful of stew, and when he'd wiped his mouth he looked over at his wife. His face kept its glum lines, but his eyes turned a bright summer-day's blue. "You got to make more allowance for a pink-haired tenor, Becky, remember that. They have it harder than the rest of us. It takes a delicate nature to climb up the scale like Oliver Bradley."

But Rebecca refused to laugh. "You can't get by me with your jokes this time," she said. "As an elder of the church, it's your duty. I'm not letting you off it."

8

THE SUNDAY AFTER New Year's, David began his series of sermons on The Christian Home. He hadn't made a visit to the Henderson house since Christmas—nothing Martha counted, anyway. He came by twice, but both times he was careful to explain that an errand had brought him; he didn't stay long enough to take off his rubbers. He was not with them for New Year's dinner. Martha invited him—not so much invited as assumed he would be there. "You're having New Year's dinner with us?" she'd said the afternoon he dropped by with the list of hymns for Sunday.

David looked self-conscious. "I meant to tell

you," he said. "I'm going to the Danielses'. They asked me a day or so ago. I'm awfully sorry."

"There's no reason for *you* to be sorry," Martha said. "We're the ones to feel sorry. I don't know what I was thinking of to let it go this late. I guess I took it for granted you'd know. Are they having a party?"

"The Bradleys, I believe."

"Oh. That should be pleasant. Just the same, I wish I'd thought to tie you down before they got to you. Why, it won't seem a holiday without you. You might have known!"

"As a matter of fact, it's probably for the best." David cleared his throat. "I understand there's been some criticism of my spending so much time here. You know how people are about their minister. They all contribute to his salary. Every member expects his share."

"Martha felt blankness settle on her. "I guess I've stopped thinking of you as my minister," she said. When David didn't speak, she rattled on. "I hadn't realized how selfish it must seem outside, monopolizing you the way we have. How stupid of me. I just hadn't realized."

"You know it isn't that," David said. He tried to take her hand, but Martha drew away from him. She felt soaking wet, drenched from the inside out.

When David announced that he would preach four sermons under the general topic of The Christian Home, his voice was grave. The subject concerned everyone present, he said, since it was in the home that what lay within the heart had its immediate reflection, giving back the light of good, casting the lengthening shadow of evil. He asked them all to pray for his guidance and inspiration as he tried to lead them out of such shadow into the light of God's will. He bowed his head for a moment of silence. Only on Communion Sundays was silent prayer a part of the service, and the congregation shifted about awkwardly before bowing with him. When they straightened, a kind of wariness had settled over the auditorium.

Up front in the choir loft, where she slid onto a chair from the organ bench after the offertory hymn, Martha felt frozen. He might have given me some warning, she thought, for she sat in profile to the congregation, exposed to their interest. She focused on the stained-glass window above David's head. Taken to the dedication of that window as a child, she'd been confused for years, having heard its name pronounced "In loving memory Henderson," between the father of her flesh, who they told her had gone to live with God, and this pink-cheeked Jesus kneeling in the purple flowers. Under the wide sleeves of her choir robe, she gripped her arms.

"The Sacrament of Marriage" was the subject that morning. The joys. The obligations. Ordained. Established. Holy. Indissoluble in the eyes of God. From the serpent of temptation in the Garden of Eden to the commandments entrusted to Moses— thou shalt not covet . . . thou shalt not commit—David came finally to the wedding ceremony, and he read it through—"till death do us part"—just before the final prayer. As Martha moved back to the organ, she could see the surreptitious rise and fall of handkerchiefs as wifely sentiment oozed in agreement.

But in the third pew on the aisle seat into which he sidled self-importantly after taking up the offering to sit as snug against Minerva as he could get, Byron Stokes's expression had turned almost as black as the coal delivered by the Stokes Coal and Ice Company of Pliny Falls. Byron left right after the benediction; he didn't go back to the vestibule but marched out the side exit, Minerva with him, red as a tomato. Minerva gave herself such a toss as she went through the door that the edging of fox on her new winter-sales' coat flirted out behind her like a tail.

The vestibule buzzed with it. On the Sundays he ushered, Byron Stokes prided himself on being the last to leave, right up to David and Mr. Higgins, who banked the fire and locked up. Byron took his ushering hard—shaking hands, slapping backs, thanking the congregation for turning out. It was good for business, he'd been reported to say, but everyone knew he had his eye on being made elder when the next vacancy came up. He never would be, not for all that he was one of the larger givers. Feeling ran too high over the way he'd carried on with Minerva and his first wife still lingering, and the way he already—only a deacon—took over in the Lord's house.

Mr. Goodall would see to it. Mr. Goodall *was* an elder, retired from the presidency of the bank, a man of dignity to suit his years, and scrupulous with the Lord: he tithed. One Sunday when Byron came up behind him and without warning landed a hearty blow across his shoulders, the old man turned on him. "If you ever dare put hand to me again, Byron"—he didn't raise his voice, but a good many people heard it—"I'll throw you down the flight of stairs out front. I warn you."

This Sunday Mr. Goodall saw Byron's departure with glee. He went over to David when the vestibule was almost empty. "Well, David," he said. "I guess your message was a little strong for some of the flock."

"Byron?" David asked, puzzled. "You don't think he was taken sick, then?"

Mr. Goodall smiled, but he answered seriously enough. "I do. In his conscience. The conscience is a mighty sensitive organ—it keeps a man jumpy."

"But Byron never so much as crossed my mind when I was preparing that sermon. I had something quite different—" David checked himself. "What would you suggest I do about it?"

Mr. Goodall stroked the blue-white loose skin of his jaw. "Knowing Byron man and boy, and his father before him, I suspect that you've done it," he said. "In all my years I've never met their equal for nursing a grudge." He was a tall man, only slightly stooped. "Anything you said you want to take back?"

"No, of course not, but I don't like being misunderstood, either."

"I doubt that you were," Mr. Goodall assured him. "I doubt that you were in any general way." He went over to the coat rack near the head of the basement stairs, and David followed; he helped the older man on with his coat. Fastidiously, Mr. Goodall lifted it at the back to adjust the hang of the shoulders. "The trouble with preaching to a specific situation," he said as he drew on his gray suède gloves, "is that you can't always know what a man may be carrying around inside himself. It's a risky business."

David set himself. That was how Martha saw him—legs straddled, head and shoulders back—when she came up from the basement. He had run his hand through his hair and it stood as stubborn as the rest of him. She felt relieved to find him occupied. She hurried out. David looked after her, and there was a pause before he answered. "If you're going to do what you think is right," he said at last, "there are certain risks you undertake."

"Well now"—Mr. Goodall had turned to look after Martha, too—"the comparison may strike you as unworthy, David, but in business you learn to measure the risk in terms of the loss you can afford. When it reaches a point beyond, you don't take it." He held out his hand. "You're young, boy. To an old man like me, you're still young."

Byron Stokes asked to have his and Minerva's letters from the church on Monday. And David couldn't shift him. Outrage had taken Byron over until there was no room left in the man for persuasion. It wasn't only the insult—it was the publicity: he and Minerva held up to ridicule, and whether David meant to or not was beside the point; the fact remained and no un-doing it. Byron blustered. "I've known well enough what they think of me!" He jerked his head in the direction of the church building down the street. "Passed over appointment after appointment, and me doing more than most of those buzzards can claim to keep the old place operating—coming through on the annual deficit, ten per cent off every ton of coal, free ice for the lemonade at the Sunday School pic-nic!" And then there was Minerva. Byron's face flushed purple in grievance. Minerva'd been through enough. There was nothing on *his* conscience. Two hundred fifty a month Sadie had cost him, and no more wife to him the last years than a stick of furni-ture—and she'd had it, two hundred fifty, all the time it took her to die. And if he and Minerva'd found a lit-tle happiness together, God knows he'd never shirked his duty to Sadie. He'd paid it to the last red cent.

"God does know, you can count on that," David said, alarmed by Byron's color.

"We don't have to take it!" Byron shouted. And it was no use David's trying to argue him out of it, he had made up his mind—they were going over to the Baptists. Minerva's heart was set; he'd given his word. Her mother had been brought up Baptist, and Minerva'd always had a hankering after immer-

sion. They could feel they were wanted there—*and*
needed. The Baptists would be glad enough to have
his help on their budget and their coal bill, and an office to fit, in return. One thing you could say for the
Baptists, they weren't the snobs the Presbyterians
were.

A month passed before David preached his second
sermon on The Christian Home. By that time, First
Presbyterian was used to the idea of the Stokeses'
turning Baptist. The jokes had settled down to
indirections like a snatch of "Shall We Gather at
the River" sung in his presence, which a man could
take or ignore, as he chose. Mr. Goodall had gone
to the treasurer and offered to cover Byron's pledge
through February, when the church closed its books
for the year. The winter's coal was in and paid for.

At the Henderson house, the weeks showed little
difference from the weeks before. The house im-
posed its routine. There were the regular weekly
meetings at church—Sunday service, choir, the
Women's League—and an occasional meeting of the
board of directors at the factory, for voting on business. Martha and Esther went their ways: together,
apart. But there was an intangible change—a sense
of things suspended, overhanging in threat rather

than in promise. Martha and David saw less and less of each other, with increasing restraint. An epidemic of flu swept through the village and onto the farms; David kept on the go in its wake, visiting the sick. Martha ached to see the lines of fatigue on his face, the darkness under his eyes, but her aching had the same quality of detachment as the days. It was as much for something withheld, beyond her reach, as it was for the David of these days. One night she wakened, crying.

And across the street, for every time that Lucy carried Esther's picture upstairs to the bedroom chiffonier, Oliver carried it down and opened it wide on the top of the still unpaid-for piano.

"The Sanctity of the Family" was the topic of the second sermon. Children of one Father, David said, heirs and joint heirs, they were members of an earthly family, too. Children, fathers, mothers, brothers, sisters. The sermon was for each according to his need. As if anyone would be put off by that, Martha thought, with all he had to say about the responsibility of bringing life into the world. About Jesus's respect and concern for the child. Oh, it was a sermon at Oliver Bradley, and there wasn't a person present who wouldn't recognize the fact. Oliver

Bradley and Esther Henderson, she acknowledged with bitterness.

Martha held her head high, but over in the soprano section Lucy's head hung down so low you could see the full length of the part in her hair, and her cheeks were sucked in; she looked gaunt. Martha suspected that she was crying. In the row ahead of her, Esther sat as unruffled as only the pure in heart have any right to look—attentive, sure. Martha begged for a sign.

The visible sign was Hattie Cornish. Poor soul, she punctuated the benediction with hysterics, carrying on to such an extent that she had to be helped from her seat and taken home by two of the men. Just two things had reached her out of the sermon: that God held parents accountable for their children, and Christ's words from the Cross—"Woman, behold thy son; son, behold thy mother"—and both of them she took to herself. And no one could convince her that David hadn't been preaching at her for giving in finally and letting Horace be sent off the year before to Willard, the state's mental hospital in the area.

"I done the best I could!" she said, sobbing. "And him gettin' heavier and heavier. Bathed and powdered and never a bedsore on him all those years. But

what could I do when he got too much for me? Fallin'
out his chair and off'n the bed no matter how I was to
prop him. Dr. Phipps will tell you, you can ast him—
and if the Reverend a been here through it all and not
just at the end, he'd be more careful how he held a
body up." She was a patchwork of splotches from
crying, her fat face sodden. "And 'tisn't as if I didn't
do for the church. Lug myself down to that basement
for the suppers, and it's always a cake or a dish of
scallop, and afterward the pots and pans, astandin'
on my feet, a great lumbersome woman and the scia-
ticy turnin' like a butcher knife with the damp. If it
was ever once to wait on the tables, in where the fun
is, but oh no, the kitchen and dishes is good enough
for old Hattie. Well, if this is the thanks I get—" She
buried her face in her handkerchief, a man's handkerchief, gray and soaking wet.

David wouldn't have had it happen for the world,
and he went straight from the church to her shabby
little four-room house. But he could no more set
things right with her than he had been able to with
Byron and Minerva. Before he left, she told him,
crying the time, that she was going over to the Baptists, where the best a woman could do wouldn't be
held against her. Tired to the bone, David laid his

hand on her head and wished her the peace of God that passed the understanding of Baptist and Presbyterian alike.

And still he pursued his series, and havoc followed each one. The last, on divorce, hit hardest. For good reason: it had the broadest target. Elaine Thompson's mother crumpled over in a dead faint, with Elaine's little boy crying "What's the matter with Granma?" Elaine's husband had left her for his secretary; the court case had been unsavory. Elaine swore afterward to a good many people that she'd be caught dead before she set foot inside the church again or sent Junior to the Sunday School. Doris Hazen, whose sister was off west getting separated from an alcholic husband who beat her, swore the same for her whole family, and there were seven Hazens in the congregation. Even Mr. Goodall took exception, either to the commotion or to something David said along the way; he went by David with a curt nod, not so much as a handshake.

The self-appointed victims came out and laid the blame on David directly, and those still neutral shook their heads and recalled that half the pulpit committee had wanted to call Gordon Jordan from Lafayette, whose wife was so good at young people's work and had been an officer in Presbyterial for two terms.

"You could excuse it if it was doin' good where the good is needed!" Mrs. Beers said in Rebecca Daniels's kitchen the Monday after the sermon on divorce. It was too cold to loiter by the fence—a day to hang the wash and run. "It's a disgrace to have the two of 'em under the roof of the church with decent, God-fearin' Christians. Why, we ought to get the law on 'em, that's what we ought."

Rebecca shook her head and brushed at the crumbs on the oilcloth of the table where they were having a cup of coffee. "I said something of the sort to Henry only the other day, but he wouldn't hear to it. 'Show me a bad situation meddling didn't do anything but worsen,' he said, and he forbade me. 'Not so much as another word!' He laid it down. 'We've done too much already!'"

"Oh, so 'twas you!" When Mrs. Beers smiled, her nose twitched and the corners of her mouth turned down in an inverted V. "We was wonderin' the other day if they wasn't somebody *behind* it all."

Rebecca tried to take it back. "An an elder, I believe Henry may have had a word with the minister. That's all. Nothing like being *behind* it. And we're out of it now. We've washed our hands. 'Who are we to judge?' Henry says. He don't believe they've actually *done* a thing. He offered to stake the mortgage on it. And you know how he is." She sighed. "No man more sot when it comes to leaving people go their own ways."

9

*B*UT HOW go your own way when the way was one you had chosen to go together? "I'm leaving!" Lucy announced. She burst in on Martha, the first time she'd been in the house since she brought the venison mincemeat—as wild-eyed as Esther just a year ago, coming out of the raw March day to meet the fact of death. Martha hurried from the pantry, where she was setting a batch of biscuit for the Annual Meeting at church that night. "I'm leaving!" Lucy said again, with such intensity that Martha felt she'd been struck.

"You aren't!"

"I am."

"Lucy, you can't."

"Oh, can't I!" Lucy was beside herself. "Just watch me!"

"Have you told anyone?"

"What difference does that make! I've told myself! I've started to pack!"

Martha took hold of Lucy's arm. She left a smudge of flour on her coat sleeve. "Wait!" she said, brushing at the smudge and only making it worse. "Wait, Lucy, I implore you! You'll feel different. Sometimes you think you can't stand something, and then when you've lived with it a while—"

"I don't *want* to learn to stand it!" Lucy said. "My God, Martha!" Martha had never heard Lucy swear, and a look of surprise crossed Lucy's face as she heard herself. "What do you think I've *been* living with! That damned picture! It's that damned picture! I could *rot* waiting. And the boys with me. *He'd* never make the move! He'd never make it one way or the other. He doesn't know what he wants even now!" Lucy's eyes were blazing bright. "Well, Esther can have him, God help her! He's not worth any more out of me! God help the two of them—they're going to need it!"

"Lucy"—Martha could scarcely speak—"have you talked it over with David?"

"*David!*" Why, Lucy's tone was as scornful as Esther's. "What does David Rathbone know about a man and woman together! What they can do to each other over a photograph! *He's* never had the guts to find out—and he won't, either, *you'll* see. The only thing David has the guts for is climbing up in his little pulpit, tearing people's hearts open with his old Thou Shalt's that he no more understands than . . . and—and climbing down again, leaving them so alive with pain they can't bear themselves. Look what he did to poor old Hattie Cornish. And Minerva Stokes, poor thing. She'll never live it down, inside herself *or* out—never, not if she lives to be a hundred!"

Martha put her hands up before her face. "Don't," she said. "Lucy. Dear."

"I've hurt you," Lucy said. "Oh, Martha!" And she started to cry. She stood straight, contorted by sobs. After a few seconds Martha moved forward and put her arms around her. Lucy clung to her. Lucy's sobs broke against her. Like Esther. Martha marveled. Exactly like Esther. Then Martha cried too. She was still crying when she went back to the pantry to throw out her biscuit dough and start again.

The news played hob with the Annual Meeting. The turnout was small to begin with, what with

March colds and all the disaffected. It hung heavy over the crepe-paper-covered tables stretched the length of the basement on their sawhorses, over the knots of the respectable gathered around the edges. Vindicated and appalled at the same time, they could talk of nothing else. Lucy nor Oliver nor Esther came out. Word had it that Lucy and Oliver were home, packing the things to go to Vermont. Where Esther was no one inquired. Martha cast silence before her like a shadow—though if anyone *had* asked, she couldn't have told them. Esther had announced that she was going for a walk, and Martha hadn't pressed her. "I know all about it," Esther had said to Martha's attempt to talk, and she wore that awful look of certitude that Martha couldn't breach.

"What's going to happen to us?" Martha's voice sounded thick from her tears.

"I don't suppose anything until Lucy has her divorce," Esther said. "Then Oliver and I will get married. Don't look like that!" She laughed, but it was not mirth; she spoke in complete seriousness. "It's always been meant. I've known from the beginning. We both have. I told you. When you feel that way at your own mother's grave!" She patted Martha on the shoulder. "Nothing's going to happen but what was meant. You'll see."

On the committee for the supper, Martha deliberately kept to the kitchen, occupied with her hands in the circle of quiet the others left round her. She hardly noticed it. Lucy's and Esther's voices buzzed in her head until her ears rang.

She was prodding the cheesecloth bags of coffee slowly coming to a boil in the two large agate kettles when David appeared at the kitchen door. He had just arrived—so carelessly put together that he looked unkempt, his overcoat lopped down off one shoulder, his tie askew. He held a sheaf of papers untidily loose in his hand. Automatically, Martha went over to him from the stove. "You couldn't do anything?"

The answer was clear from his face. The stubborn assurance was gone. He looked middle-aged. He shook his head.

"Then it's definite." As if she hadn't known that morning.

"It's definite."

"When?"

"As soon as Lucy can get off, she says."

"What does Oliver say?"

"Nothing. It's Lucy."

"And there wasn't anything you could do?"

"There wasn't anything I could do."

"Oh, David, I'm so sorry."

"*You're* sorry!" David said.

The whole kitchen had become still and Martha realized that the women at the stove and counters were straining to hear. "Do you think I should go along home?" she asked in a low voice.

"Why should you?" David looked down at his disordered papers rather than at her. "I have to see Jo Thompson about the treasurer's report. I intended to spend the afternoon. . . ." He shrugged, and his coat lopped back another inch. Then he did look at her and his voice lost its indifference. "Don't go," he said. "Please. I need to talk to you after the meeting."

So she stayed, and when the business of the supper and the year was cleared away David drove her home, and they sat for a time out in the car, with his old moth-eaten army blanket tucked around her knees. David sat half facing her, his elbow resting on the steering wheel, his head on his hand. His back was toward the Bradley house, which stood against the evening like a checkerboard; from cellar to attic, every window was a square of light. "Of course I'm going to resign," he said.

It was the one thing—the obvious—that hadn't occurred to her. She looked at him dumbly.

"I've failed here," he went on in the same tired, flat voice. "I've failed these people."

And suddenly Martha felt taken over by hope, light as air with it. "Do you have any plans?" she asked. Her blood seemed to stop as she waited for his answer.

He was quiet for a stifling time. "No plans," he said, not lifting his eyes to hers. "Just to get away. To try somewhere else. The church can get a substitute until they find a new man."

Martha could feel her blood pounding against her eardrums.

David read his resignation at the end of service the next Sunday, with a brief statement. He looked over the faces of his people lifted to him, criticism in abeyance, affection showing in incredulity and protest, and he broke down. With both arms raised to pronounce the benediction, he stood arrested, unable to say the words. He shook his head once, as if shaking might clear it of regret, but he couldn't speak, and when the silence had gone on too long Martha played an Amen softly on the organ, and she began immediately the arrangement of "Faith of Our Fathers" that she'd chosen for the morning's postlude. She played it over and over, until the church had emptied and she could turn off the organ and put her head down on the keys.

Esther came to her finally—Esther, not David. "I'll make it up to you." Esther spoke like a child offering another child a present. "Come along, honey." She took Martha by the hand and pulled her to her feet. "We'll make it up to you, Oliver and I."

David did come to Martha, the evening before he left. "I have to see you," he telephoned to say, urgent. For a second there was that terrible lift of expectation, but she knew better. She dismissed it at once.

David wouldn't let her give him back his mother's locket. She had it waiting on the mantel in the drawing room, where they sat, the few minutes he was there, facing each other. "I feel you should take it with you," she said. She put the box into his hand.

He let it lie on his palm "Why?"

"It means so much to you. The associations you have with it are so dear."

"My associations here are dear." He returned the little box to her hand and he left his hand on hers, pressing it slightly. "I shall like knowing that you have it."

High in her throat, Martha's heart ticked off the seconds; it throbbed against his hand on hers. She ran her tongue over lips. They throbbed, too. "When I can't have you?"

There was a pause before he spoke. "My conscience will never be at peace again for the part I have played in bringing this about," he said. His voice sounded as if it were addressed to some invisible listener. "I feel I have betrayed my calling. I could not go on living with myself if I were to reap the fruits of that betrayal."

"And I am your atonement?" Martha said.

He seemed to be thinking. "You could say that. I would say my sacrifice." David's pressure on her hand tightened, then he let it go. Like that, he took himself from her.

Martha's tongue stuck to the roof of her mouth, it was so dry, and when she spoke her words came out almost as dry. "Poor David," she said.

But after the door closed on him, she stumbled back toward the den. She hit her thigh against the corner of the drop-leaf table; she struck the edge of the doorframe, misjudging space. Out by the couch, she dropped to her knees. "Now I lay me . . ." It was all that she found in her mind. Not another word. After a while, giddy—like the earlier death—she got to her feet. Her knees had stiffened, her shoulders hurt. When she passed the mahogany framed mirror built into the wall, she saw the pattern of the crocheted afghan marked deep into her forehead.

In the drawing room, beside the chair where he had sat, Martha found David's handkerchief. She held it up to her face. Not very fresh, not very fine. "Oh God," she said into the shabby handkerchief. There had been tears in his eyes at the door, hadn't there? She washed and ironed the handkerchief that very night, before she cleaned the silver. "Oh, we keep busy!" she said once aloud, in the pantry, and she worked straight through, with the moon. "Nice things deserve care." That was Mama, and Martha carried the handkerchief and locket upstairs with her at last and put them in the bottom of her handkerchief box, with a fresh sachet of lavender on top. And when she went to bed in the early morning, she slept.

There were no letters—there was no word. Sometimes Martha's heart took over her senses and she would look up, thinking she saw him coming toward her, his smile all light because she was there. At night she wakened in pain so sharp that she could not be still but would sit on the edge of the bed, rocking from side to side in a denial of his desertion, unable to make real the fact that he had not loved her enough. One night she heard herself grunting. Women grunted like that in childbirth, she'd been told, but what had she to deliver? A stillbirth of hope? Of love?

10

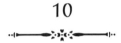

*O*LIVER and Esther went to a justice of the peace in Auburn to be married, just the two of them, and a small notice in the Auburn paper was the only announcement that was made of their marriage. They came back to the big house from their honeymoon; there was never a question of their going anywhere else. They moved into the big square front room that had been Emmeline Henderson's—into the mahogany bed with its massive carved headboard that rose up the wall halfway to the ceiling, into the chiffonier, the dresser, the wardrobe, the closet, the fine old Victorian secretary beyond the fireplace to the south. Family pictures lined the man-

tel and covered what wall space was free: Martha and
Esther through the stages of their growing up, their
father framed in wide chased silver, their mother—
her train sculptured into careful folds in the fore-
ground—the center of a vast bridal party. They
moved into Emmeline Henderson's history: bride,
mother, widow. Every piece of furniture stood where
she had placed it, every picture. While Esther was
away, Martha had put new curtains at the windows
and dressed the bed with sheets and blankets that had
never been used, but she had not moved a thing. "We
can move the furniture around whenever you want—
however you like," she said when she accompanied
them to the bedroom door.

"I don't want anything changed," Esther said.
"This room means everything to me, exactly as it is,"
and Oliver said that was all right with him, just so
long as he had somewhere to hang his hat.

"Until we have pictures of our own babies to put
up," Esther said. "Then I might feel different."

"I'll fix myself a place in the den," Oliver said. "If
you ladies will be good enough to give me a piece of
the roll-top desk, that is."

Martha laughed at the way he said "You ladies."
"Of course you must have a place of your own for all
your business things, Oliver," she said. "We'll empty

the desk first thing Monday—why didn't I think of it myself! You'll be using Mama's secretary, Essie, and I'll take the library table in the parlor. The den can go back to being the office!"

As Martha had aired her mother's room the day before and taken the English linen sheets from the cupboard, she put bitterness aside. How could you breathe air weighted with punishment and not be cast down? The house had felt like a sepulcher those days that Esther was away—haunted by endings. Martha imagined it returned to happiness. Laughter. A family. The village would accept, given time. They could wait.

When Esther and Oliver arrived, the rooms shone in welcome. Though there were just the three of them for dinner, the table was set with the best damask, with the gold-and-white china, the gold-banded crystal, the old English monogrammed flat silver, and the heavy silver serving dishes—all brought out rarely and only for parties of special importance. There were flowers, and the two tall Georgian candelabra held ten new beeswax candles. While Esther and Oliver unpacked and changed, Martha finished the dinner preparations, and when they came down, the table was ablaze with light and festivity.

Esther stood in the wide doorway, her arm tucked

into Oliver's, and her eyes filled with tears. "Oh, Marty," she said, "you went to the vault."

"I did. This is a wedding party. I didn't see why we shouldn't have one, even if it is a few days after the event. There's champagne, and a proper wedding cake for dessert." Martha motioned to the head of the table. "Oliver must sit here," she said "This will be his place from now on. In Mama's chair."

But Oliver refused. "No," he said. "Thank you for the honor, Martha, but I'd rather sit beside you where I can look across at my beautiful new wife." He pulled out the Hepplewhite armchair at the head of the table for Martha, and went to the side chair at her left and held it for Esther, who was waiting. After he had seated her, he kissed her lightly on the top of her head. "If you remember, Lucy always did the carving at our house," he said as he went round to the third chair, at Martha's right.

Inside, Martha winced. "Whatever you like, so long as you feel it's your home. That's the important thing," she said, and they talked of the places Esther and Oliver had been on their seven days away—Lake Placid, Fort Ticonderoga, a stop to look at Niagara Falls. It was not Esther's idea of a honeymoon, but Oliver was adamant about its being something he could pay for, himself, and what with the divorce and Lucy's weeks in Reno, which he had had to borrow on his life insurance to pay for, there was very little to spend.

Martha had considered giving Oliver a check for a wedding present. She had decided against it, and instead had had twenty-five shares of the Henderson Preserving Company stock transferred to his name. It seemed appropriate, since Oliver would be going at once into the office there. "To look after the family interests" was the way Martha and Esther put it, though not Sid Corbett's way. Oliver had already closed out his insurance business, and it was fitting that he should join the company a stockholder.

Esther and Oliver had returned on a Saturday. "Will you be coming to church?" Martha asked them next morning at breakfast.

"And why not?" Esther swooped like a hawk, though earlier Martha had heard her singing upstairs. "Oliver and I are man and wife, and they can take it or leave it."

"In the sight of the law," Oliver said, and he laughed. "That's what may stick in their crops."

Esther turned on him. "And just what do you mean by that?"

"Nothing in particular. Keep your feathers dry. I was only thinking that the sight of God may be more what they have in mind. God made manifest in man." He laughed again. "Sanctimonious buggers—begging your pardons."

"Oliver!" Esther said.

Martha spoke quietly. "In the sight of the *family*," she said. "That's what will count in the end. You'll see. In the sight of *this family*."

Martha left early, as she always did, to get into her robe and be at the organ, with the music for the service laid out at hand, by ten-thirty. Neither Esther nor Oliver had sung in the choir since Lucy left town with the children, and Oliver had not been in church at all. But as the final bell tolled from the steeple and the minister began the invocation—"The Lord is in His holy temple. Let all the earth keep silence before Him"—Martha saw them slip into a back pew off the center aisle. Not the side aisle, she thought approvingly. The center. Esther looked stunning in the new suit and hat she had gone off to be married in. Her head was high. Oliver held his head ducked a little, but he was very smart, with a richly patterned silk handkerchief showing at the breast pocket of his jacket. They left the church with the pronouncement of the benediction and got away before anyone could speak to them—or choose not to.

"I see Esther and Oliver are back," Mrs. Bowles said to Martha when she came down the steps from the chancel. "Tell them I'm sorry they didn't wait round long enough for Willis and me to say congratulations." Willis Bowles was the minister who had followed David—an older man, whom everybody liked enough and no one liked too much. He seemed kindly—after all, he had come to bind up the wounds—but divorce was beyond the stretch of his acceptance; he had told Esther that he could not in conscience marry her and Oliver. They might be able to find a minister who would, he couldn't say as to that, but so far as he was concerned it was impossible to give their union the blessing of the church.

"I'll tell her," Martha said.

"We'll be around to call one of these days," Mrs. Bowles said. "I wouldn't want them to think that just because Willis couldn't marry them they don't have our personal blessing, because they *do*." She squeezed Martha's arm in a propitiating gesture.

"They'll look forward to your call, I'm sure."

"We both wish them every happiness. Will Oliver be going into the factory right away?"

"Oh, yes," Martha said, pulling herself loose. "It's why they had to cut their wedding trip so short. We're coming into the busy season. He's needed."

Oliver took up his new position on Monday. Office Manager was the title that had been arranged for him, and a small square had been partitioned off the secretary's quarters, with beaverboard, to give him a place. It took two windows from Miss Piper's light, and her cross ventilation. Miss Piper had a sharp head for figures and a sharp tongue to go with it. Besides, she had known Lucy in the Book Club and admired her mind. The reception Oliver met at the factory was cool.

Esther waited at the side door when he came in a few minutes after the five-o'clock whistle had blown over the town. "Well, how did it go?" she asked before he had the door closed behind him.

"Fine," he said and he gave her a perfunctory kiss. "Peachy dandy."

"Was everyone polite?"

"Polite! Are you out of your head? The boss's husband and a holder of twenty-five shares of the company stock? I made the rounds and I told them straight, 'Watch your step around *this* new officer of the preseve if you want to hang onto your jobs!'"

"Oliver, you didn't!"

"That was a small joke, hon. Old Sourpuss Piper never let me out of my box after Sid did a quick tour of the plant for my benefit and turned me over to her. 'Mr. Bradley, you should familiarize yourself with the production schedule'"—he was a good mimic—"and in she came with half the office file and dumped it on my desk. 'Mr. Bradley, here are the shipping orders. You should be up to date on those,' and in she came with the other half. If she'd had her druthers, I'd have gone without so much as time off for lunch, but the whistle blew and I ran for it. She was busy setting out a peanut-butter sandwich on a doily on her desk or I'd never have made it past her. If you think that whistle's loud here, you should be under it sometime. It's enough to blow your brain through the top of your head. I took off like the startled hare."

"Peanut butter!"

"A manner of speaking—I didn't risk stopping to check. 'There's too much to be got through in *this* office to go out for *lunch*' was as close as she came to letting me in on it. It's a good thing I have a reliable bladder. It's sure as hell going to be put to the test."

"Oliver!"

"Just a statement of fact—no vulgarity intended. One of the realities of life as Office Manager, as I see it after a day." Oliver yawned. "Do you think I could stretch out on the couch for a few minutes before dinner? Is there time?"

"Don't you want to come up to the bedroom? You'd be more comfortable."

"But less apt to sleep, sweet. This will be fine. Anyway, I'm not sure I could make it up the stairs. That day was as long as a month of Sundays under old Dr. Westcott."

"Of course there's a lot to learn," Martha said at dinner—Oliver at her right, Esther at her left. "No wonder you're tired. You get to bed early and have a good rest. Who did you have lunch with?"

"Stan Harmer and George McGregor—the boys."

"Oliver," Esther said when they had gone to their bedroom. "I didn't want to say this in front of Martha, but those men you had lunch with—they're not the people you should be associating with."

"'Associating with'! Sweet Jesus, who do you think I am?"

"The Office Manager of Henderson Preserving, for one thing. My husband, for another. Things have changed for you. There are social distinctions, and the sooner you learn them, the better. And you'd better watch your language—we aren't used to it. Those are not people we would dream of having in this house—they or their wives."

"I wasn't having lunch with them in this house. I wasn't even having lunch with their wives, pet. We happened to be at the Busy Bee at the same time, and we sat down together and broke bread."

"That's not the point."

"There's a point?"

"Oliver, please. We have ambitions *for* you if you haven't any for yourself. You might remember that Martha and I *own* that company now Mama's gone— seventy-five per cent of the stock. Office Manager is only the first step. There's no reason you shouldn't be vice-president in another year or two."

"Have you let Sid in on that? Or Sourpuss Piper? Or what's his name, that fathead from Rochester? For God's sake, come to bed. What do you think I married you for, anyway?"

"Well, I hope for more than *that*." But she unpinned her hair and flirted it over his face. "Oliver?" she said later, in a soft, wheedling voice. "Will you do something for me—something that really matters to me? Will you come home to lunch?"

Oliver made a sound that might have meant anything.

"I've been thinking. There'll be a vacancy on the bank board when Mr. Leland dies. He's had his second heart attack, you know. There's no reason you shouldn't have it. The bank needs someone younger. It has to be someone of substance. If you're highly enough placed in the company, you'll be the obvious choice. You have a position to live up to now. I'm not just thinking of myself. I'm thinking of our children. I want them to have a father they can be proud of. Oliver, do you hear me?"

"Don't you think it's awfully quiet here?" Oliver began to say in the evening. Cooped up by the clock in his beaverboard square, in the unaccustomed silence in the empty, unaccustomed space at home, he was restless. He wandered from room to room, with nothing to do once the paper had been read and left strewn beside the Morris chair except a ride around the lake if the weather was fair or an occasional movie in Geneva. There wasn't even choir rehearsal to break the week's monotony.

"It will come," Martha said. "Just be patient. You'll be asked to come back." But they weren't. Willis and Evelyn Bowles made their call, bringing their personal blessing and a piece of rock from the Holy Land, but there was no mention of choir or of singing. The visit was short. And Oliver and Esther no longer seemed interested in singing at home, though Martha suggested it occasionally.

Every Sunday afternoon, Oliver settled down at the roll-top desk and wrote a letter to Teddy and Bud. He had written the first one the Sunday after they went away, anguished at the gash their going had made in his life. Nothing had prepared him for the finality. He had not prepared himself. He sat down at the rickety table in the room he was renting at Mrs. Hislop's boardinghouse and opened a pad of lined paper he had bought at the drugstore. "Once there was a raccoon who had a fox for a brother," he printed in careful block letters. "No one knew that they were brothers, because they didn't look like each other except that they both had pointy noses. *They* knew they were brothers, though, and they used to laugh because they were the only ones who did. The raccoon had black rings on his tail and a black mask on his face. The fox's tail was long and bushy, with a white tip. The fox was the big brother and the raccoon was the little brother. It didn't matter which was which. They took care of each other. They were different in all their ways. The raccoon slept through the day, curled around himself in a warm circle, and the fox watched to see that no hunting dogs got near enough to harm or frighten him. Of course he also trotted around. After all, he had slept through the night and was rested, and he was curious to see the world. The fox waited until it was getting dark to hunt for his supper, and when he had eaten and his stomach was full, he went into his burrow and lay down to sleep. His tail curled up in front of him. He could put his head on it, like a pillow. At night, the raccoon liked to go on adventures, in gardens and garbage pails mostly, but he never went so far that he couldn't get back to his brother the fox to poke him with his pointy nose and let him know if there was a dog out looking for him. Together, they were smarter than any dog. They didn't need anyone to help them. They were happy because there were so many things to do, lolloping through the woods and fields around the gardens and garbage pails, and they had each other."

Oliver read it and cried. It wasn't much. Lucy could read it to them or not, as she chose. At the bottom of the last page, he made small drawings of a raccoon and a fox. They were both smiling.

That was the only kind of letter Oliver could seem to write to the little boys. Sometimes the brothers were a woodchuck who lived in the ground and made tunnels and a squirrel who lived in a nest of leaves in a tree and did his traveling overhead. Whatever they were, they went their own ways, but they always protected one another and acted with unfaltering devotion. In no letter was there ever a mention of a mother or a father. The brothers of the letters were sufficient unto themselves and the day and each other. They were never lonesome for *anyone.*

The Sunday after his first week at the factory, Oliver sat down with his lined pad. "Once there were two brothers," he wrote. "A monkey and a kangaroo. The kangaroo was the big brother and the monkey was the little brother.

'I smell trouble,' the monkey said. He had a very fine nose for that sort of thing. 'Someone is shut up in a box.'

'Can't he get himself out?'

'No, he is a prisoner.'

'Did he do something bad, do you think?'

'Bad enough to get shut up in a box, that's for sure.'

'Pretty bad?'

'Worse—terrible.'

'Then I guess we better leave him alone. He probably needs to be punished.'

But the little brother was softhearted. 'I expect he wishes he hadn't done it,' he said. '*I* think we ought to go get him out.'

'Oh, all right,' the big brother said.

With that, the monkey jumped into the kangaroo's pocket, sniffing to guide the way, and the kangaroo leaped ahead as if he had on seven-league boots.

'I wish I could cover the ground the way you can,' the little brother said.

'I wish I could climb trees and swing from the branches the way *you* can,' the big brother said back. 'And smell things far enough ahead to have an idea what I'm getting into. I just *go*, and sometimes there I am, up in the air bounding one way when all of a sudden I know it's the absolutely wrong direction and it's too late to change.'

'I guess each of us has our own particular talent,' the little brother said.

'Well, let's not make a sermon out of it,' the kangaroo said, putting his little brother in his place.

The little brother didn't notice. He was too excited. 'Slow down, we're almost there. Straight ahead is where I think.'

What they stopped at was a long, three-storied building made out of yellow bricks—very ugly.

'That's an awfully big box,' the big brother said. 'You can tell it's a prison all right.'

'I'd better see what's what,' the little brother said, and he hopped out of the kangaroo's pouch and shinnied up a drainpipe to the first floor. It was high. 'He's here,' he called down, 'but it looks like he's stuck in a box in a box. I don't think I can handle this by my-self—it's too much. Is there any chance you can bound your way on up?'

The big brother jumped until he was winded, but his talent was for distance across, not distance up, and he kept missing the window by at least a foot. Besides, there wasn't any way he could stop himself in the middle of a bound. Even if he'd got the right height, he would have whizzed past.

'Too bad!' the little brother called in to the man in the box in a box. 'We came a long way, but I guess there isn't anything we can do for you.'

'I guess not,' the man in the box in the box said. 'I guess maybe there isn't anything *anyone* can do. I've done it for myself. But thanks a lot for trying.'

'That's all right,' the little brother said. 'So long,' and he settled himself into the big brother's pouch and off they went, back to where they had come from."

A kangaroo and a monkey both smiled up from the bottom of the page. They were in mid-air, and they looked as if they were flying.

11

*T*HE WEEK after he started coming home to lunch, Oliver bought a console radio for the den that was called the office once again, and he kept it roaring from station to station. He was always on the lookout for something else than what he had. It got on Esther's nerves. "Turn that thing down!" she would call from another part of the house.

"What's that?" If he knew what she was saying, he never let on. Sometimes he even got up from his chair to go to the hall to ask.

"*Down!*" she'd call in a fury. "Down! Down! Down!" and she'd lift her hands to her head, distraught.

Oliver always turned the radio down, but no sooner had he changed to another station than the volume seemed to rise of its own accord. Martha sometimes wondered if he didn't use the radio to drown out things she and Esther couldn't hear.

"Do you think Oliver is happy here?" she asked Esther.

"Happy? How should I know! What's happiness got to do with it anyway!"

"He gave up a lot for you, Essie."

"*He* gave up! *He!* And what about me, I'd like to know!" Esther spoiled for a fight, and neither Oliver nor Martha would ever oblige. They retired before her, took themselves out of the situation.

"Oh?" was all Martha said to that, and she went to the kitchen to make a batch of penuche. Martha moved from snack to snack these days. They were beginning to show on her hips, in a thickening waist.

There wasn't any need to ask if Esther was happy. She wasn't. It registered on her face. Esther wore a closed-in look, and her eyes asked a perpetual question—not of Martha, not of Oliver, but of something outside them all. Everything she undertook she started in a whirlwind, to drop, unfinished, for long spells of brooding, sitting idle, her eyes wide with her question and set on something far away.

Esther didn't have enough to do. No one coming in, no place to go—the town continued to ostracize them. Courtesy in public, but private doors closed. Except for the visit from Evelyn and Willis Bowles and an occasional dinner with Sid and Hortense Corbett, there had been no callers in the house since Lucy and David went away. Not even Rebecca Daniels dropped by as she used to. She was warm and friendly with Martha out in the yard, and as friendly with Esther as she had ever been, but the line was drawn there; she no longer came into the house. "I'm sorry, Martha," she said one time, "but there's some things as can't be countenanced. It isn't any judgment on *you*, but that's how a good many of us feel."

"Those old harpies don't bother me!" Esther said, but the days were so long, they were so much alone. "It will be different with children," she said. She talked of it constantly—what they would do when the children came.

One noon, Oliver came into the kitchen, smiling. "Well, hon," he said to Esther after he had kissed her. "I'm on my way at last. Those children of ours are going to have a father to be proud of in spite of himself. You're looking at Treasurer Bradley of the Building Fund Committee for the YMCA that our town fathers have set their hearts on. Office Manager Bradley of the great and only Henderson Preserving Company, first step. YMCABFC Treasurer Bradley second step, Vice-President Bradley in another year or two, and a seat on the bank board whenever the good Lord sees fit to act. To him that hath shall be given! Just a little death and destruction in the right place and his upward path will be up and up, to say nothing of over."

"Oh, stop being so silly! Esther said. "It isn't funny. Anyone would think you didn't have the wits you were born with."

Oliver's good nature was unbreachable that day. "Who's to say? Who's to calculate? I wouldn't presume."

Martha, over at the stove, had laughed. "I think it's wonderful," she said. "Pliny Falls *needs* a Y. And the Building Fund is very appropriate for you to be the head of. Why, it's an honor—a building!"

"I don't know about honor," Oliver said. "But 'appropriate' hits it right on the button. You two had better get ready to cough up for the cause. Why else do you think they asked me? Only I'm not the head, Martha. If we're honest about it, just the three of us gathered so happily in the kitchen for lunch, I'm the bookkeeper."

"It's an honor just the same," Martha said. "To be trusted with the books! Mama used to say that when you came down to it, that's the ultimate trust! We'll be glad to make a generous pledge, won't we, Essie."

"Who's going to be chairman?" Esther asked.

"Of the Building Fund Committee? Byron Stokes."

"Byron *Stokes*! Did they say why they weren't offering it to you?"

"Now, now, let's not be greedy. Little steps for little feet, remember. Byron's already made *his* way to the board of elders of the Baptist Church, if you'll recall. Far beyond even my own ambition. Or you might say he delivers the goods to more of the town's establishments and has a larger public to appeal to, influential as is my post in the preserve."

"And kindly stop referring to the company like that. It isn't dignified."

"Sweet," Oliver said, "hasn't it occurred to you yet that dignity is not what you married when you married me? For God's sake, it will give me something to *do*. How about eating early tonight? We're having a meeting in Byron's office to get the thing organized."

The five members of the Building Fund Committee met in the office of the Stokes Coal and Ice Com-

pany two evenings a week. Building Fund was the title, but moving and renovation were the realities. Mr.
Leland had offered a large, sound, unused stable on
his place. The only condition he put on the gift was
that it be moved from his land. Madame Lovett would
give the land to move it to. *Her* condition was that the
money for the moving be raised by the town. The
land she was ready to give was almost two acres in
size. There would be space for the stable, a parking
lot, and for outdoor tennis courts if a group was
willing to build and maintain them. When it came to
the plans of the committee, there were no conditions
—they drifted into dream. Complete gymnasium
equipment. A basketball court. Bowling. Perhaps in
time a boathouse. The land was on the outlet. Com-
petitive bids for moving the stable, solicitation of labor and materials, the collection of cash for what
could not be donated were the topics of the evenings'
agendas, but more than half the time the men spent
together went into talk that had nothing to do with
the YMCA or the recreational needs of the young
people of Pliny Falls. And Oliver and Howard Jami-
son and George McGregor stretched it further with a
stop after the meeting at the Coffee Shoppe of the inn
or the Busy Bee, where the doughnuts and pies were

made on the premises. Oliver returned home late those evenings, though never so late that Esther was not waiting up for him.

After the boredom of the office and the dismaying quiet of the house, Oliver's life freshened. One night he came in singing "My Wild Irish Rose," and without getting out of his coat he took Esther around the waist and waltzed her in a circle to the music of his own singing across and up and down the wide hall, from the foot of the wide, curving staircase and back.

Esther laughed—a rare sound those days—and the two of them went up to the big front room with their arms around each other, Esther singing the melody while Oliver sang an improvised descant, sweet and clear.

Three weeks later, Esther missed her period. She came down to the kitchen one morning after Oliver had left for work and she threw her arms around Martha. "I'm going to have a baby!" she said. "Look, I'm crying."

Martha held her tight. "Oh, honey," she said, "don't *cry*!"

"Tears of joy," Esther said. "Tears of earthly joy."

For thirty-six days she was radiant. Snatches of *Messiah* followed in her wake as she went about the house. And then the blood came and the baby washed away in its warm flow.

Esther acted like a creature gone wild. Martha had to call Oliver to come home from the factory to help calm her.

He took her in his arms. "You mustn't carry on so," he said. "It isn't good for you. Of course it's a terrible grief. It is to me, too—do you think I don't want a child? But only two months—why, he wasn't even a little fish yet."

Esther wrenched herself from him. "He was to me," she said. "He was the fulfillment of my life."

"There'll be another," Oliver said.

She shook her head once, slowly, and began to scream.

"Did you hear Miss Esther carryin' on like a banshee yesterday afternoon?" Mrs. Beers said to Rebecca Daniels over the fence beyond the cherry tree.

"I did," Rebecca said. "She lost the baby she had her heart set on. It's a long time since I've put foot inside that house, but you can't be neighbor and not go when there's trouble, no matter what they done. There was Martha and Oliver, white's a pair of sheets, and Esther screaming her head off. I gave her a good hard slap each side of her face—it's the only way—and she turned to moaning and whimpering and Oliver went off with her upstairs and got her to bed, I suppose. I didn't stay to know. 'I'm sorry I had to do it, and after all this time,' I said to Martha, and Martha told me what it was was the matter. 'We have to pray there'll be another,' Martha said. She looked pretty shook up. They won't be if I know anything— not to term. Her womb's flighty, just like the rest of her. She's not built to hold onto them—but it didn't seem the thing to say, not under the circumstance, so I left it that they was to call if they should need me, and I come along home. Martha was going to the telephone to call the doctor."

"I see him come," Mrs. Beers said. "He was there a while." After a pause she added, "The Lord giveth and the Lord taketh away."

"Well, I expect 'twas Oliver did the giving," Rebecca said, "but it may well be the Lord had a hand in the other. Who's to say. That's not a happy house, Elivra. You can feel it in the air—that air feels kind of curdled."

"And why wouldn't it be?"

"Poor Oliver," Rebecca said. "Lucy was the back-bone of *that* house. He can't hope to handle what he's got on his hands now—he hasn't got it in him. Home nor to the factory neither, from what I hear. And his own kiddies lost to him."

"He should of thought of it before. There's consequences to be met in this life, Becky, when you fly in the face of God's own law."

"Rebecca nodded. "There is. I don't dispute you there. But it don't make it any easier when the time of meeting comes and you have to take them on. Trouble is, we don't have a sure way of knowing what consequences it is we're laying down for ourselves. Even though he done it to himself—and he did, no one else—I feel kind of sorry for Oliver. I don't think he had a notion in the world what he was getting in for."

"You're soft, Becky, that's what's the matter with you," Mrs. Beers said. "He deserves every bit of it and more."

Dr. Roberts, who had taken over Dr. Phipps's practice, was concerned about Esther. He saw her every week. He gave her pills for her insomnia. And Martha suspected him of speaking to Mr. Bowles at the church. One day Mr. Bowles telephoned to ask if he could stop by to discuss something with Esther. He came that same afternoon. What he wanted to discuss was whether she would be willing to organize a nursery department to entertain the little children downstairs during the morning service. He'd had the idea for some time, he said—it was asking too much of the tiny ones to sit quiet through the sermon and a good deal of a minister to preach over the disturbance that they made—but the right person hadn't come to mind until he'd suddenly thought of Esther. Would she consider doing it?

"Oh, they wouldn't want me, the mothers wouldn't!" Esther told him with a toss of her head.

"I think they would," he said in his easy, matter-of-fact way. "Let me talk to some of them and see." And either he or the prospect of being free for an hour overcame whatever reluctance the mothers may have had: Mr. Bowles came back to tell her that she had been quite mistaken. They would welcome her. He would like to know her decision as soon as she could give it to him. The sooner the better.

"But what about Oliver?" Martha asked when Esther said she'd decided to do it. "Have you talked it over with him?"

"If Oliver can leave me to go off on his Building Fund jaunts two nights a week, I guess I can leave him to contribute *my* services for a single hour."

"But it's church."

"Oliver can go alone. He used to go without Lucy when she had to stay home with the children."

"That was different. He had his place in the choir. He was needed. It wasn't the same at all. A man goes to church with his wife. He's not likely to go without you, Essie."

"That's up to him," Esther said. "It's his business, not mine. I don't have choir, either. *Or* the Building Fund. Maybe it's my turn to be needed."

Oliver chose not to go to church. He stayed home with the *Syracuse Journal*, and Esther went off to the basement Sunday School primary room, where the youngest children were deposited with her before the service started. It proved the very thing for her. Esther was at her best with little children and the paraphernalia that accompanied them—with stories and songs and crayons and blunt kindergarten scissors; she had the patience for them that she lacked for everybody else, and deftness at maneuvering scarves and leggings and boots. And the children adored her. Of course it was only for an hour. She came home the first Sunday shining with eagerness and affection for the world she had just left. Martha saw it with amazement. She turned to Oliver to share her delight and caught on his face an expression so naked with wist-fulness she felt chilled. She launched into an account of the sermon, which had been dull, and every time Esther tried to go back to telling of the children, Martha cut her off.

It was a season of harrowing. On Children's Day, not long after, Lucy telephoned from Vermont, ostensibly for Teddy and Bud to talk to their father. It was over two years since they had left. Oliver could not even picture with sureness what his two sons looked like. They spoke into the telephone as if they were speaking to a stranger—self-conscious and shy. Oliver felt shy speaking back. He could hear Lucy prompting them. "Letters," he heard her say.

Teddy said that their mother read them the letters he sent. "Did you know Bud and me are brothers?" he asked. "But not like those brothers. We fight. Bud beats me up and I beat him up."

Oliver said he supposed that was the way it was.

"But we don't hurt each other," Teddy said in a virtuous tone of voice. "Just sometimes."

"That's good," Oliver said. "Sometimes is often enough."

"Well, good-by," Teddy said. "Here's Bud."

"Hello," Bud said in a faraway voice.

Oliver said, "Hello Bud, what's going on in Vermont?"

Bud didn't say anything. Oliver could hear him breathing—light, quick: a child's breathing.

"How's Billy? Does he like it up there?"

"I guess not," Bud said. "He died."

"I'm sorry," Oliver said.

"We had a funeral," Bud said. There was another pause, and again Oliver could hear his breathing. "We have a surprise," Bud said then. "We're going to get a father."

Oliver heard Lucy's voice in the background once more, and Bud said, "Mommy wants to talk to Aunt Martha."

Oliver called Martha. It was the first time Martha had heard from Lucy. Lucy sounded like the old days, full of energy and projects. She had a job she liked. But the big news was that she was going to be married—to a widower in Rutland, with two children of his own and a farm where they could spend the summers. He wanted to adopt the boys if Oliver would give his consent. The lawyer would be writing him about it. "I think it's best," Lucy said. "They're at the stage where they need a firm hand, and the four children get along. He's a very fine person. Very responsible. He would like to give them his name. And Martha, another thing—when that all goes through, perhaps it would be better if Oliver stopped writing. Maybe you could suggest it."

"Writing?" Martha said.

"Those letters he writes every week or so to the boys—about the animals."

"I don't know anything about them," Martha said.

"Oh, never mind, don't mention it, then. I can just stop reading them. The boys hardly remember him, you know, they were so young. I haven't talked to them about him—they couldn't possibly understand how it was. You couldn't expect them to. I have a hard enough time myself. We feel it will be better all round if they start over fresh with another father. Oliver won't need to send any more money, obviously—but the lawyer will go into it all." Lucy laughed. "I've gained ten pounds—what do you think of that? Tell Oliver, will you? I don't want him worrying about us. We're all well and happy."

Long after she had hung up the receiver, Martha stood staring through the telephone box on the wall, and when she came on Oliver, his head on his arms across the roll-top desk, his body shaken in sobs, instead of tiptoeing by she went to him and laid her hand on his shoulder. "It's the balance," she said. "It's only the balance"—not knowing exactly what it was she meant but hearing in the words some overtone of truth.

12

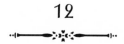

AT THE Henderson Preserving Company, business was booming. It was booming all over the country. The last week of the year, before the books closed, a bonus beyond the regular Christmas bonus was declared. "It'll be on the government," Sid Corbett said at the directors' meeting at which it was voted, "but the help don't need to know anything about that. We might as well get the good will out of it on the side." At the next quarterly meeting, in the spring, it was decided to build an addition to the plant, to be able to handle the increasing number of orders coming in. With the space they had, they could barely keep up: string beans, carrots, cabbage, tomatoes, corn; fruit as it ripened. At the height of the growing season, the women in their white head scarves and long-sleeved, enveloping aprons were working double shift. Too little space—that was the problem. They would have to expand or turn down business. And then Sid Corbett had his ambition set on working out a method for drying potatoes. "There's a fortune in it once we get it licked," he said so often that ears he was saying it to stopped listening, and he took a section of the top floor of the factory for his experiment. The failures and their stench were on a matching scale, but his determination never lagged. With the right equipment they would get it: that's what was needed—more modern equipment and room to set it up and operate it. And more space for shipping. "God knows, they need that," Oliver reported at home. "The corridors are lined to the ceiling with cartons ready to go. You feel as if you were walking through a tunnel. I go through in a crouch." He imitated himself. "I can see the day coming when they'll have me really holed in and I'll have to go out by the drainpipe."

"But where would the money come from?" Martha asked at the meeting. "We don't have that kind of reserve as I read the report."

"We'll borrow it," Mr. Latham said.

"*Borrow!*" Martha said. "But that's debt. Henderson's has never gone into debt. 'Debt is the mother of folly.' If I've heard Mama say that once, I've heard her a hundred times."

Esther declaimed in her elocution voice,

> *"Neither a borrower nor a lender be;*
> *For loan oft loses both itself and friend*
> *And borrowing dulls the edge of husbandry.*
> *This above all: to thine own self be true—"*

Mr. Dowling interrupted. "Yes, yes," he said smoothly. "Those were highly commendable old saws—sound principles, that is to say—but business practice has changed since your mother's day, Martha, as she would be the first to grant if only she could be here with us. A forward-looking woman, always. These days, husbandry is a very different thing from what it was in Bible times. Then it was a matter of conserving what you already had. Now Lord knows I'm a conservative—I've never voted outside the Republican Party in my life, and never expect to—but enterprise is what makes good husbandry today. Looking ahead and planning for what you see. Preparing yourself to take advantage. Using your credit. This is a growing country. More people every year, and the one sure thing we know about them is that they all have to eat. More money to spend. The banks know it. This company is as solid as the Rock of Gibraltar, and they know that, too. It's *safe*. We'll have no trouble getting whatever financing we want, and no trouble paying it off. As a matter of fact, I've taken the liberty of doing some sounding out. No trouble at all, I can assure you. '*Carpe diem*,' if you'll allow me a quotation of my own." He cleared his throat. "That's the motto we should be operating on today: '*Carpe diem*.' I assume that everybody here remembers his Latin."

Around the table, nods confirmed his assumption.

The financing proved as easy as the men had predicted. Applications were put out and accepted. Contracts were drawn up. Notes at the banks in Syracuse and Rochester, where the company had always done its business, were signed and countersigned. There was a ground-breaking ceremony, with the help and the officers and the directors grouped around Martha and Esther, their hands on a spade with a ribbon tied in a bow to its handle. Afterward, a sterling-silver miniature of the spade, engraved with the date, was presented to them by the contractor, to commemorate the occasion. Work was begun.

Even Oliver was drawn into the excitement of change. He had never felt anything but alien to the

office and for that reason was overscrupulous in ob-
serving hours and office rules. Now by choice he left
the house early in the morning to check on the prog-
ress being made by the big machines and their crews.
As Office Manager looking after the family interests,
he conferred almost daily with the contractor. When
he came home, he reported in detail how the schedule was proceeding, and more often than not he
drove Martha and Esther to the plant after dinner, to
see for themselves. In the general spirit of expansion,
he bought a new car—so much down, so much a
month. Martha and Esther agreed that the right thing
had been done.

The addition was almost completed by the time
the Depression came to disprove them. The Crash
brought the first warning of disaster: word that Hurl-
but Thomas, the New York broker whose connection
with the company went back twenty-five years, had
put a gun in his mouth and blown himself to eternity.
His office addressed the telegram with the news to
Martha. She called his wife at once. The stock market, was the most she could learn. Speculation. It was
a time of incoherence; there wasn't a clear answer
to be found anywhere. Rumor spread from the radio and reading of daily papers until a sense of ca-
lamity pulled Pliny Falls taut. And then, as work

went on, and pay envelopes for the workers, the taut-
ness eased. Except for the few owners of stocks and
bonds, the Crash became an aberration of the world
outside.

But over the stretch of months that followed, business at the factory showed a change. It was gradual:
smaller orders from some of the brokers; requests by
others to defer payment on orders already filled; future orders canceled.

"We'll weather it," Sid Corbett said confidently,
but his lips seemed to grow more pinched by the
week. "We're going to have to lay off some of the
help," he came by the house one midafternoon to an-
nounce. "Now I mind as much as you do, Martha," he
added fast, not giving her chance to speak. "I know
what it means as well as you do, and probably a hell
of a lot better—pardon the language. But we're in as
deep as we can go on credit. The water's deeper than
I think you realize. Don't argue with me. I know
what I'm talking about."

Martha and Esther began to understand when the
banks moved in on the company loans, which, it
turned out, were callable. The factory itself was the
collateral against which they had been made, and
Rock of Gibraltar though it might be in normal
times, in the times they were in what the banks re-

quired was cash. The tone of the letters was regret-
ful—associations were long and valued, but their
own necessities controlled the decision. The bank of-
ficials had looked ahead and could not risk the future
that they saw. Six weeks was as long as payment
could be put off. The letters in Mr. Latham's hands
trembled as he announced the news to the other
directors.

After a month of desperate consultation between
lawyers and representatives of the banks and a final
fatalistic study of Miss Piper's books, they had to let
the company go. There was no alternative. Even Sid
Corbett agreed, and if ever a man was a die-hard, it
was Sid.

Northrup Products bought it. Ed Northrup was on
his way to becoming one of the shrewdest men in
upstate New York. In his late thirties, with an air of
authority about him, tall and powerfully built and
driving toward success, he was a man who played
business with joy, like a game to be fought hard and
won. He moved in on the bad times with vision and
with capital enough to convert it to action. Small
family-owned factories like Henderson's were a part
of that vision. He had acquired two in the area
around Pliny Falls when he installed in one of them

equipment with which to manufacture his own cans. Cutting a thin margin of profit from the tin, he was able to undersell his competitors until, having undersold them to the breaking point, he could have them at his price. Only companies with accumulated assets that could keep them going, selling at a loss until times changed, could hold out against him. When it came to Henderson's, Northrup presented the alternative between bankruptcy and sale. He had liquid capital to pay off the bank loans plus a token amount for the stock, and Henderson's Preserving Company became a unit of Northrup Products before there was time to comprehend what had happened.

Martha and Esther voted the controlling shares. How could they refuse, knowing the certainty of foreclosure, with jobs gone the length of Main Street and the narrow streets than ran each side? Foreclosure and disgrace. There would be no place for Oliver in the new organization: that was made clear at the final meeting with the Northrup representatives for the signing of notes and papers. The beaverboard partition would come out first thing. Ed Northrup planned to change the sales staff and the brokers and the management as quickly as he would change the labels on the cans. The only executive to be kept on was Sid Corbett, and Sid's title was done over to meet what the Northrup chief lawyer from New York called "the challenge of the times." As Manager of Production, Sid's first responsibility was to hire back all the men and women workers at a fifteen per cent cut in the pay they'd been getting. Without a break, the factory would go right into beets. The canning season was near its peak.

Oliver in the middle, Martha and Esther each side, like a trio of sleepwalkers they came home from the meeting. In Emmeline Henderson's day, the business would have been brought to her, to the office and the roll-top desk at the back of the house. Challenge of the times or no, she would have suited the hour to her own convenience, and its termination—not answered a lawyer's summons to appear and sign and be dismissed. The thought filled Martha with a greater sense of defeat than she had felt when the pen was put into her hand by that pompous man from the city, who wore his pince-nez on such an expanse of wide black grosgrain they looked as if they had been conferred on him. "We had no choice," she said. She turned, anxiously, and for half a dozen steps walked sidewise. "You agree, don't you, Oliver? There wasn't anything else we could have done?"

"What's it going to mean?" Esther asked in the same portentous tone she'd been asking the same question since Mr. Latham had made his first announcement to the directors.

"There wasn't another thing we could do, was there?"

"That's right," Oliver said. His mustache was as clipped and debonair as ever, but he looked drawn. His face hung in folds, he was so thin. He chewed at his lower lip.

"This is the end!" Esther said.

"Now girls!" Oliver dabbed at his mustache, as he did when he was about to make a joke. "Don't forget that you still have a man in the house!"

Esther swung around to face the other two. "We won't lose the house! We haven't signed away the house!"

Martha shook her head. "The factory never owned the house, Essie. The house was no part of that enterprise for the loans. There just won't be the money for upkeep. We must be sure to call Mr. Hughes first thing tomorrow to cancel the order for painting and the new roof. Not that he won't know without being told. It's too bad we didn't have them done three years ago, when we first talked of it."

"Oliver will have to paint," Esther said.

"I don't know about that," Oliver said. "A job as big as this house takes professional equipment."

"You can begin with the pillars," Esther went on. "They look the worst. The plant has all kinds of ladders and equipment. Sid can send over whatever you need."

They had reached the steps of the porch. Oliver stopped. "Let's get one thing clear, right now. I'm asking no favors of the plant. Now or ever!" His voice shook. "Not if my life depended on it! And the same goes for my wife. Is that clear? Not one damned thing!" He took out a cigarette. His hand was so unsteady that he used three matches before the flame and cigarette met.

"As you please," Esther said. "But those pillars are going to be done if I have to get out there myself. They're a disgrace to the name of Henderson!"

"And what about the name of Bradley!" Oliver shouted. He threw down his cigarette and stamped on it. Then he sagged. "I'll do them, I'll do them, for God's sake. Only quit nagging me!"

"You don't have to shout—I hear you," Esther said.

Martha intervened. "Oliver will have to be looking for a job, Essie." They were at the front door,

home again. She made a little sound with the inflec-
tion of laughter. "We can't expect to make a house-
man of him yet!"

To celebrate their take-over, Northrup Products
staged a parade. Ed Northrup honored it with his
own presence, riding between the mayor and Sid
Corbett in the back seat of a touring car, just behind
the high-school band and the National Guard carrying the colors, and ahead of the American Legion,
the Veterans of Foreign Wars, the Shriners, Rotary,
the Masons, the Boot and Saddle Club from Geneva
on their high-stepping mounts, the Boy Scouts,
the Fire Company augmented by a hook-and-ladder
from Newark, the ladies of the Fire Department
Women's Auxiliary, a bagpipe band brought in from
Rochester, and floats at the end, to be judged and
awarded prizes at the loading platform of the new addition to the factory, where bunting draped the po-
dium that had been erected, and the Northrup insig-
nia loomed large back center. A carrousel, a Ferris
wheel, a tent for serving refreshments had been set
up on the cindered area between the factory and the
railroad freight yard.

Martha and Esther and Oliver debated at length
what attitude they should take toward the celebra-

tion. Ignore it? Undignified. Attend? Unbearable. In the end, they decided to watch it in a public way. They would not be in hiding; it could be borne. Early in the morning, Oliver hung out the flag on the horizontal pole over the pillared porch and brought three folding chairs to the front of the lawn. Ten minutes before the parade was scheduled to start, they seated themselves. They sat with fixed faces, lifting their hands in greeting to the occasional passerby hurrying toward the factory grounds, while the music of the high-school band and the skirl of the bagpipes gradually grew louder and then gradually faded, and finally Oliver said, "I guess they must have changed route and turned down Green Street—not come this far up Main"—and they folded their chairs and went into the house. Oliver laughed so hard he threw himself off balance and landed against the doorjamb of the vestibule.

13

ⒸLIVER opened an office over Butch Parker's barbershop. Real estate. Jo Thompson had taken on his old office next the bank, along with the insurance firms Oliver once represented. The upstairs room was cheaper, and a good location; he could keep in touch with the boys and gather leads by just dropping in downstairs. The Building Fund Committee no longer met. Until things picked up, there was no more money to be collected for a YMCA or pledged against a future as fearful as the one that seemed to lie ahead. Mr. Leland's stable sat on his land where it had been all these years, and Madame Lovett's land remained a meadow. Oliver had a

neat sign lettered—*Oliver Bradley, Real Estate*—to hang in his window, and cards printed with his name and office address and telephone number, which he distributed in the mailboxes in town and out along the rural routes. Esther worked with him, addressing envelopes; it took days. All through September and October he drove hectically about the country, examining properties and showing them to possible clients. It was a life with movement, more suited to Oliver's taste. But everyone wanted to sell, not buy, and what the clients he drove around seemed to be after was to satisfy themselves with what they had. During the entire fall, he made only one sale—a small house to an old man on a government pension.

"It's the time of year," he said. "Fall's never the season for real estate. People won't buy in the fall. Stands to reason. Heating bills. Snow. All this"— he waved vaguely—"is groundwork I'm laying. Groundwork's what pays off in the end. That's one damned thing I learned in the insurance business. Watch me, come spring!" He waited out the winter. And in the spring he looked to summer, then to fall again and further groundwork to be laid, while the bill at the garage grew longer and longer and the unpaid office rent accumulated until he couldn't see Butch without making some reference to it.

"Better than having her empty, eh, Butch boy? Nothing runs down the value of your property quicker than to lie idle—I'm the man who can tell you! But I'll have it, you can lay your bottom nickel on that. It's this damned buyers' market," he explained to whoever might be down in the barbershop. "People who don't know where their next meal's coming from aren't out to buy property. It's the times. It'll shift—has to. Things can't go on like this. The country won't stand for it." He talked darkly of the government. "Well, by God, I'm going to beat them at their own game. I'm hanging on if it kills me!" His manner outside was jovial and optimistic, however tight-lipped and morose he might be at home.

"But what are you using for money?" Esther asked regularly.

"I'm getting along." He was short with her. "You let me do the worrying about *that*."

The pillars were painted as high as Esther could reach, standing on a chair. The face of the house looked as if bangs had been cut across it, low. Even that amount of fresh paint showed off how dingy the gray had become, the cracks in the shutters where the slats had dried out. It was over ten years since the house had been painted. But there was barely enough income now for taxes and food and for coal. When it rained, they had to remember to check on the tubs set under two leaks in the attic—the trunks were pulled into a huddle in the center to be safe in case they forgot and the tubs should spill over.

They learned to be careful. Leaving unused rooms closed and without heat in the winter. Turning off lights. The spring after they lost the company, Esther put in a garden. Mr. Daniels suggested it. "Ah, there's nothing to compare to the feel of it, Esther." He kept his eyes on the earth sifting through his hand as he crumbled a clod with his fingers. "This is good soil. It'll never let you down in the way of men, or your own heart maybe—given decent care, that is, and some patience with God." He measured off the plot against the lie of the sun, and he came over after supper and on weekends to help her with spading and planting and steady, encouraging advice. He was the one person who had never been different since her marriage, though once trouble came everyone was friendlier. And it was obvious that Oliver would have all he could do to keep up with the grass, off as he had to be through the country when the green things grew fastest.

It turned out to be a wonderful garden. "Oh, life's good!" Martha said to the first lettuce and radishes, and again when Esther brought in peas and tiny new potatoes for the Fourth of July. They ate a diet of vegetables and homemade bread, with eggs and cheese instead of meat, and they canned the fruit cellar full that used to be stocked with cases done up at the plant to their special order.

There was less time and energy for the house. The vacuum gave out and there was no money to replace it; the carpets covering the floors were too heavy to drag to the line without the help that had always been available from the factory. "Why fuss?"Oliver said. "It looks all right to me!" Martha and Esther gave the curtains an airing and washed the kitchen cupboards and let the fall cleaning go by with scarcely a qualm. And it seemed to Martha at harvest time, with the altar stacked for the service with pumpkins and squash and with tawny shocks of corn brought in from the farms, that she had only once before approached a winter with a greater sense of Thanksgiving.

Esther felt the same. "You can laugh if you like," she said as they were leaving the church, "but I feel kin to that altar."

14

AT THE BEGINNING of the new year, Byron Stokes and Roger Bates from the Building Fund Committee of the YMCA called on Oliver to ask for his resignation as treasurer. At home. Without even what shelter of privacy his grubby little office might have provided his pride. Byron announced that they'd come for the books. Oliver was slow to comprehend. He thought they wanted the latest figures, for outlining a possible campaign for the new year. "Sure, sure," he said, leading the way through the house to the den. "I have it all right here. Keep all this stuff at home. It's been a bad year—why not?—but most of the pledges are in:

twenty-two hundred smackers and some change the last I totted it up. Not bad, considering the general state of the village purses." He opened the top right drawer of the roll-top desk and brought out a ledger, with the payments and pledges entered in neat columns.

"I'm afraid you don't get the point," Byron said. "Didn't mean to put it to you quite so frank, but the plain fact is the men feel it ain't fair to you *or* the organization to throw you in the way of temptation with public funds like that, not considering what *you* owe—the town practically carrying you. Hate to have to come out like this, but that's the long and short of it, and maybe it's doing you a service letting you know how people feel. Not that I've got any personal complaints, understand. Your coal bill's always paid on time. I wouldn't want to lose your trade over this."

Oliver had turned so white around the lips that a thin line showed beneath his mustache. "Let me get this straight," he said. "You thought I'd stolen your damned money, is that it?"

"Well, let's put it this way," Byron said. "We thought if you was to keep on like you've been going since you got thrown out at the factory, you might be tempted and that's the truth. It's for your own protec-

tion is how you want to look at it—see?" He turned
to young Roger. "That's about the size of it, wouldn't
you say?"

Roger's Adam's apple bobbed above his collar. He
looked like a man with a chokeberry in his mouth and
no place to spit. He shuffled, lifted one shoulder,
shrank into his collar.

"No hard feeliings," Byron added.

"You bastards!" Oliver said. He sat down at the
desk, took out the Building Fund checkbook, and
with a hand so shaky his signature ran off the line he
wrote a check for the total sum in the account. The
paper rattled as he held it out, stiff-armed, for Byron
to take. The ledger and checkbook he thrust at
Roger. "Now get the hell out of this house. Fast." He
was shaken by such anger that his bones felt as if they
were no longer held together by a center.

And he wasn't given a minute to catch himself.
"What did those men want?" Esther came right at
him. "What did you mean, letting them let themselves out like that—not going to the door with
them?" She grabbed his sleeve as if she might pull the
answer from him. "What have you *done!*"

He pushed her aside to go to the hall, but not before she had seen the open empty drawer. She followed him. "It's *money!*"

"Not money in a way you'd know anything about." If she hadn't seen his lips moving, she might not have known it was Oliver speaking; his voice had no body.

"Tell me!" she demanded. "Something's happened! I have a right to know. Oliver, I'm your *wife*!"

"God knows I'm not forgetting that," Oliver said. "I'm going out. You'll know when I get back. I promise."

"Will you be gone long?"

"Not long." She had moved over close to him again, and he gave her an absent-minded pat. His little mustache stretched in the caricature of a smile. "Don't look so scared," he said. "I'm all right. You might say I'm all righter than I've been in a good long time."

"I don't believe you," she said flatly. She stood undecided while he got his coat and galoshes from the hall closet and went to the side door.

"Cheerio!"—that same empty voice as he went through the den.

When she heard the door shut after him, she rushed to open it. "Oliver!" she called. "Do you want me to come with you?"

He didn't answer, and foreboding took her over as she watched him back the car out of the garage. It reached the street and she whirled and ran upstairs to the sewing room, where Martha was stitching side hems in the sheets she had turned that afternoon. "Something's wrong!" Esther called. "I feel it in my bones! Something terrible's happened!"

"Whatever are you talking about, Essie?" Deliberately, Martha went on tying threads at the end of a seam. She peered over the top of her glasses to get Esther in focus.

"If you could have seen his face!"

Martha dropped her sheet. It fell in a rumple all around her. "Whose face? What is it?"

"I shouldn't have let him go." Esther wrung her hands. "Oliver! He wouldn't tell me. After those two men—it had to do with those two men. Like death. He was! And don't go trying to talk me out of it. I *know*."

Martha was on her feet now, too, at Esther's side by the window, though there couldn't be anything to see. That window looked out the back, over a stretch of snow-laden fields patterned with tree shadows, black flickering on white.

They went downstairs, switching on every light as they went, and they stood by the tall, narrow windows at each side of the front door until their legs were stiff with cold. But it was impossible to sit still for more than a minute. At the sound of a car, Esther rushed back to the window. It wasn't Oliver. It never was. "You'll wear yourself out," Martha said, hurrying after her. "We'll hear him the second he turns into the drive."

"I can't stand it any longer," Esther announced when three quarters of an hour had passed. "I'm going over to see Roger Bates."

"Oliver won't like it!" Martha warned her.

"You stay here in case they try to get us on the telephone."

"Who on earth would be trying to get us at this hour?" Martha said. They both spoke as if they were short of breath, though neither would put words on what it was she feared.

"I don't know"—Esther settled her hat securely—"but they might, that's all."

"If he comes while you're out, I'll call the very second."

"He isn't coming," Esther said. "If I thought he was, I would hardly *debase* myself by going to Roger Bates about it!"

"Debase yourself! Why, Roger Bates is a nice enough young man."

"He and that Stokes devil are back of this—you can't tell me!" Esther slammed the door behind her.

Martha paced the hall while she waited. Esther was back in less than fifteen minutes. "We have to get hold of the State Police!" she called ahead of her; she flung the big door the full stretch of its hinges. Her face was as white as the snow she brought with her. Roger stood outside on the walk. She jerked her head in his direction. "Roger's going to get some of the men together." Her voice cracked.

"Mrs. Bradley, I can't tell you—"

Esther swung round on him. Because of the steps, their eyes met level. "What harm did Oliver ever do to you!" she said, her weight tipped back on her heels, her head thrown back, in outrage. "What single thing did he ever do to a one of you!" She wheeled from him and ran for the telephone.

"Oh, God," Roger said. His feet fumbled in the snow. "I guess I'd better hurry. We're meeting at the post office, to cover the roads." Still he stood uncertain. "Believe me, Miss Henderson," he said to Martha, who was waiting, shivering, to close the door, "I wouldn't have this happen for—" He shook his head. "We'll do everything we can to find him. Believe me. Oh, God," he said as he ran down to the street.

The State Police found Oliver collapsed over the wheel of the car, the engine going, a length of hose attached to the exhaust. He was in a coma but not dead. He must have spent most of the time since he'd left the house driving around the country, they thought; the car was warm. They rushed him to Auburn City Hospital, where he lay, his head encased in an oxygen tent, like an animal in a cage, unmoving except for the slight lift and fall of the bedclothes that covered him. Esther and Martha kept vigil at his side, and Esther never cried once—not until Dr. Black, the Auburn doctor, told her that they had given Oliver back his life but there was nothing they could do to give him back his mind; it was lost to the carbon monoxide.

Then Esther retired into tears, made a refuge of them, using tears to hide behind. Remorse? Strain? Or the humdrum fact of having to pick up and go on. Martha couldn't tell. If only David were here, she caught herself thinking, grief looking back to grief and the comfort she had known in him through the anguish of her mother's death those years ago. The present was more difficult—the present turned up with each day's light like a fresh fall of snow or a misting of dew cast wide on the fields: newness laid over the top of time, and what went before still underneath for its reckoning.

Martha took on the present. She ransacked the

drawers and pigeonholes of the roll-top desk for unpaid bills, and when she had them together, all ac-
counts long rendered and some with repeated pleas
for payment and some with threats of collection
agencies and a recent dunning letter from a finance
company, humiliation swept her in waves, like nau-
sea. She added the sums that were owing and felt de-
spair at the amount. When they didn't know where
the money for the medical expenses was coming
from!

They sold the car. The few days more that Oliver
was in the hospital, Esther made her daily trips to
Auburn on the bus. "For the little *we'd* use it now that
Oliver won't be driving," Martha explained. "And to
tell the truth, we need the exercise." She patted her
hips. But the car money was soon gone. Evening after evening, she covered pages of the company's old
letterhead with figures that might show a way
through the morass of Oliver's debts, given time
enough and going without. The roll-top desk was lit-
tered with them—her mind, as well—but never with
the way.

The way came to the door. Madame Lovett
brought it. Martha was almost too surprised to welcome her in—Madame Lovett, who these days but-
toned herself into her old cobblestone house with the

first skim of snow. Young Jo Berryman brought her, in the long black Cadillac they kept for funerals, and he handed her to the door as delicately as if she had been a client. "My thanks to you, young man!" She ordered him away with a roar, coming in on her cane and a hand held out to Martha to hoist her up over the step at the threshold. "You may return in an hour, if Martha here will put up with me so long."

She stopped in the hall for Martha to lift off her cape. "Light, isn't it? That's the advantage of fisher. 'Buy fisher, Laura,' my dear mother used to say. 'It's *light!*' I'm leaving it to you, Martha, and you ought to have it for next season, Lord willing. I don't like this outliving myself, it's indecent—and I'm telling you now because I want you to *wear* it. I've never been one to set myself above the creature comforts. It'll outlast the two of us."

She rocked along to the drawing room and, creaking and groaning, she lowered herself into a chair. "Now, what I want to hear is, how are you girls planning to manage?" With the blunt end of her concern, she poked at Martha. "Speak up!"

"Why, we're going to sell the house." Until she said it, Martha hadn't known, but on the instant she saw it as the solution.

"Just what I thought!" Madame Lovett's wrinkles

deepened with her satisfaction. One of the few pleasures left her, she said, was to be right. "I've come to
take out a mortgage on it. Want you to *keep* it." When
Martha's perplexity showed on her face, she added,
"Cash, girl. Cash! Well, what do you say? Speak up!"
With the volume undiminished, Madame Lovett's
voice somehow gave the impression of softening.
"You can draw up a mortgage form if you like, Martha, but now I've got my last will and testament out
of my system I'm not so much for the signing of papers, if you could see your way clear to humoring an
old mummy like me. What do you say to forty-five
hundred? About do it? Don't like to see one of the old
places go out of the family," she said quickly, as if to
parry Martha's gratitude. "Have to do what we can to
keep up the tone of the county! It's not what it was.
That new crowd with their blooded cattle—talking
about raising colts for the Saratoga sales! No background. Nothing but money, and most of that more
than likely down the drain if you could get at the
books. Your mother was very dear to me. If you'll
just hand me my bag—I have a bank check with me."
She reached into her alligator satchel and brought
out an envelope and laid it on the table at her side.
"See you don't lose it!" She ended the subject.

Over Oliver, she shook her head. "Too bad. Too

bad. Always enjoyed the man's singing at church," she said, "which isn't to say one way or t'other about him as a husband. Never did get round to calling on that first wife of his. Meant to, and I was sorry when there was all that ruckus—felt out of it. But I was brought up in another age. 'Let 'em wait, Laura,' my dear mother used to say. 'Let 'em wait.' I've known her let 'em wait a lifetime. Oh, well." She peered at Martha. "Ever hear from your young man?

Martha shook her head, thinking that if she were to laugh she would cry and if she were to cry she would never come to the bottom of the tears. "Not directly!" she shouted.

"He wasn't half good enough for you, Martha!" Madame Lovett shouted back. "Standing there in First Church under that beautiful Tiffany window and telling us how to conduct ourselves in our bed-rooms! You were well rid of him. You have your home. That's what matters."

Early next morning, Martha went to the bank, and after the check was deposited she made the rounds of the stores, the printer's, the garage. She went to Butch's last.

"I don't like to take it from you, Miss Henderson," Butch protested. "Like Ollie was always sayin',

makin' his little joke, it was better him and not payin'
than havin' the place run down from layin' idle."
Even though she argued, he would accept only half
of the accumulated rent. "Gosh, we feel awful about
what happened," he said. "As if we was all to blame
somehow—not seein' what was goin' on in his life.
We thought a lot of Ollie down here, and that's a
fact."

At home, changing to go to the city, Martha moved
lightly about her bedroom, humming louder and
louder until, without conscious thought, she burst
into the words of "Praise God from Whom All
Blessings Flow." She took the afternoon bus to Auburn, and she went straight to Oliver sitting in a chair
in his hospital room, a blanket over his knees, and she
took his limp, unresponsive hand in hers. "You don't
owe a penny!" she told him. "Not a penny!" She lowered her face close to his, as if that might press home
the marvelous news she had brought. "You aren't in
debt to a soul. Not to one of them, do you understand? Not any more!"

He nodded and smiled—but he always did when
Martha was nearby.

Oliver could leave the hospital in another day.
Everything was ready at home, the big front room

upstairs aired, the curtains at the windows there washed and ironed, a floor lamp carried up from the back parlor. Martha was in a mood for planning how and where and what, but she got no response from Esther. Esther grew quieter by the hour; she scarcely spoke beyond a monosyllable. And that evening, in her long-sleeved flannel nightgown, her hair in a braid down her back, she came into Martha's room.

"Marty, I'm not bringing Oliver home," she announced in the old defiant air, so familiar except that there were lines across her forehead now from her habit of raising her eyebrows at life, and lines running from each side of her nose to her chin, from fatigue. "I can't face it."

Martha looked up from her dressing table, unbelieving.

"Dr. Black says he can get him into Willard if that's what I want. I talked with him about it today."

"*Willard!* But Oliver isn't out of his head like *that!*"

"They take all kinds," Esther said. "Dr. Black says he can be committed, there'll be no problem about it."

"But does Dr. Black *want*—Does he think Oliver would be better off?"

"He says it's entirely up to me." Esther's voice

rose. "After all, Marty, he *did* try to kill himself!" She covered her face with her hands; the easy tears washed through. "I should have let him go—that's what I live with! Alone with him in that awful, ugly little hospital room—you don't know what it's been!" All the time crying. "He *wanted* to go. If only I hadn't interfered, he could be at peace at last."

But Martha had had tears enough and to spare. "Rubbish!" she said. "Stop talking such rot! Oliver's at peace. Look at his face, how it's all smoothed out. His face is perfectly happy. And *he'll* be, with the two of us to take care of him."

"That's only your idea," Esther said through her hands. "It doesn't make any difference to him where he is. He doesn't even know!"

Martha tingled to her finger tips with anger; her heart raced with it. "He knows more than you think!" She stumped over and turned down her bed to get herself under control. "He'll be better with time, you'll see," she said in a calmer voice. "You're just tired, and no wonder—the shock, and every day like that. Here." She brought Esther a clean hand-kerchief.

Esther dried her tears. "I'm *not* just tired," she said. "And you can talk till you're blue in the face, I'm going to do it. I *know* it's right."

"Sometimes you know too much for your own good!" Martha snapped at her. "Put that in your pipe and smoke it." She hadn't used those words to Esther since they were children. But it was no satisfaction. She didn't sleep.

Next morning, Martha got up early. She went down the back stairs quietly and, without stopping for breakfast, she put on her boots and heavy coat and wrapped a long wool scarf about her head and neck and went for a walk in the winter half-light before Esther could come down and ask questions. Esther was having her coffee when Martha walked in the side door. Snow and all, she tramped through the den straight to the kitchen. "You can't," she said abruptly.

Esther raised her eyebrows. "Can't what?"

"Send Oliver away."

"But I told you last night, it's all decided. As a matter of fact, I told Dr. Black yesterday. After all, Marty, *I'm* Oliver's wife." Esther set her cup down with a bang. "Who says I can't?"

"I say it. And Mama says it. I've just been out to the cemetery."

"You haven't!"

"I have. I thought if it helped you so much when you were making the great decisions for all of us, it might help me. It did. I found out just what was meant. We're to keep Oliver here. It was as clear to me as it was to you that time—"

"But Marty—"

"Almost as if Mama was speaking to me!"

"But don't you see, Marty"—Esther pushed her chair back from the table; she gripped the edges of the seat with both hands. "She *wasn't*! It must have been your imagination! She couldn't have been! It was just that I was so determined I thought she was! It couldn't have been meant. That's the whole point—it couldn't. Look what it's led to!"

"I've been looking," Martha said to that. "My God"—Lucy a shaft across memory—"what else do you think I've *had* to look at all these years! Now *I'm* determined. And I'll tell you something. If you go ahead and do this anyway, I'll sell my share of the house and leave town. And that's a threat. I'll not have Oliver sent away! I'll not have it, do you hear? He's paid enough."

Martha stood in the puddle that snow had made around her boots, the very image of her mother.

15

OLIVER WAS LIKE a child. They tended him like a child. And contrition—or shock, or the need for punishing assuaged, perhaps—turned the town to kindness. There weren't enough chores to mete out to the offers of help. Roger Bates stopped Martha on the street one day. He wore the same plaid cap he'd worn that night at the house. Under it, his face reddened with bashfulness. "I know Mrs. Bradley don't want to see *me* for a while," he said, "but I was wonderin'—maybe later, come spring, I could put in her garden for her. I'll be puttin' in my own—no trouble. I'd sure appreciate it if she'd let me."

"That *would* be good of you, she'd be grateful,"

Martha assured him. "We both would. It will be a relief to her to know. We keep pretty busy these days!"

Rebecca Daniels and Mrs. Beers insisted on doing
the laundry for a while. "We're all carrying a load on
our consciences you got to let us work off" was the
way Rebecca put it, and every few days one of them
called for the sheets and towels.

Mr. Daniels came to sit with Oliver, quietly smok-
ing his pipe. Mr. Daniels would say it had been a
good day, or a bad—whichever suited the weather.
They sat companionably in their own repose and
self-possession.

Once Oliver was home, Esther cared for him without complaint. It was as if she had found the answer
to her question and now must live it out. Between
them, she and Martha kept him immaculate. His hair
had turned a silver white. When spring came and he
could be out of doors, it gleamed in the sun from their
brushing. "There!" Esther would say, giving a pat to
the white linen handkerchief she had folded and
tucked into his pocket, as spruce as the one he used to
fold himself.

No doubt of it, Oliver was a credit to them, removed to a world of his own but gracing theirs with
dignity and acquiescence. In time, he puttered a bit
about the place, among the flowers. And when the

Little Hill for Little Voices was under way, he could take part in the recitals, watching the unfolding and folding of young Berryman's chairs, standing at the door, and from his corner seat in the front row—so well kept—nodding encouragement to pupil and parent alike, unstinting.

Martha and Esther started the Little Hill for Little Voices the year after what was generally referred to as Oliver's accident. The need for money was a steady pressure. What else were they equipped to do? The first fall they announced it, they had eight pupils enrolled, and the number had grown over the years. Esther gave lessons in comportment and elocution; Martha taught piano. From September through May, on late afternoons and all day Saturday, the house vibrated at the front with scales and exercises, with "The Happy Farmer" and "Für Elise," with "The Rustle of Spring"; at the back with children's voices raised in monologue and declamation.

It was on a teaching day in spring that they learned of David's death. Rebecca Daniels came over at noon with a letter from her cousin in Lake Placid that told of it. Rebecca was old. She moved heavily, impeded by fat and rheumatism and some kidney trouble that puffed her ankles out and over her shoes.

RACHEL MACKENZIE

"A cerebral hemorrhage," she wheezed. "Imagine! Why, he couldn't of been—how old *would* he of been, Martha?"

"I haven't any idea," Martha said. As long as she lived, he would be forty-two, fixed in time.

Rebecca settled onto a chair like an old hen nesting, spread out around herself. "I hope the news don't upset you, Martha. I thought you'd rather know than not. Odd he never married," she said after a bit. "Too set on his mother is the way I always figured it. Nothing ties a man down tighter."

In on the piano bench with Georgia Parker, Butch's youngest, Martha went through her teaching from some automatic surface level. Thoughts of David engaged her at a distance. Her feeling about him was comfortable, not grieving. In the hour and a half since Rebecca's visit, David had been restored to her. Death had given him back. "So they say!" She dismissed the cerebral hemmorhage to herself, while aloud she counted out "The Minuet in G." For Martha knew better—all that suffering! David had died of a broken heart.

She sent Georgia off to Esther in the den and crossed the room, stopping to straighten the paisley shawl that covered the shredded velvet of the couch, adjusting the square of monk's cloth draped over the

THE WINE OF ASTONISHMENT

wing chair by the black-marble mantel. Not a chair but had its square of material like that, tucked around the seats and hanging in points over arms and back, where the upholstery had gone. And the paper was giving way, too. In spot after spot it hung out from the wall, curving wide. The rooms had a ghostlike quality—the loops of paper, the points of fabric, the fraying fringes of the lamp shades all set in motion by breeze or opening doors or footsteps. And yet it was home. What did it matter that sun and dust had taken their toll on the curtains? Martha stood between them in the long side windows where she could see Oliver in his chair, and her heart lifted in love to the spring outside—kin to the fulfillment of tulip and daffodil and the froth of blossom breaking over the cherry tree, as Esther had once felt kin to the harvest.

She nodded to the truth she had found. It was Oliver's gesture, and wondering at the quiet of his face without its smile she went out and down the back steps to the cherry tree where he sat, his hands slack on his knees. "We mustn't be sad!" she leaned over him to say. "David always wanted the best and now he has it!"

Oliver nodded, but he didn't smile.

"See!" she said, and she smiled. "I'm not sad,

Oliver—I'm happy. And I'll tell you why. When you've known a love like David's and mine, it's . . . forever. What's time? And Oliver," she went on in the soft murmuring with which she talked to him, rather like talking to herself, "I've had such a wonderful idea! Standing here, with you. You know the snapshot of David I have, put away in my drawer upstairs? I'm going to take it to Auburn and have it enlarged and framed. We'll hang it over the piano!" She took Oliver's hands in hers. "David loved music— remember how the music in church always mattered to him?" Oliver nodded, and Martha let go his hands and reached up to break off a sprig of cherry blossom to tuck in her hair. She touched it gently. "We can keep his memory green at recitals!"

The sun through the cherry petals dappled, then danced over their faces as they smiled and nodded together.

And so they did, at the year's big recital late in May shortly before the close of school. "We must make it an occasion," Martha said to Esther. "Something very special." It took days to find the thing that would be special enough. "No, that doesn't speak to me," Esther said to idea after idea. But in the end it came, and they went to the trunks in the attic for Mama's oldest clothes so carefully folded away. The recital would be costumed. "Not a word to a soul!" Martha said as they ripped and pressed. "We must keep it a surprise!"

Surprise was certainly what the children felt when they arrived on the bright May afternoon at the side door, a half-hour early, to be met by Martha, regal in long black taffeta, its gussets and seams let out to receive her, a high boned collar of net rising toward six of Mama's bonnets mounted in a pyramid on her head. "Sh!" She laid a finger to her lips and pointed the way to the den, where Esther, wearing Mama's wedding gown—stiff with embroidery and bones, deepened to the color of old ivory—waited for them with other dresses and with pins: elaborate curving bodies; sweeping skirts of twill, braid-trimmed, of heavy patterned silk; a collection of bonnets laid out on a table.

There wasn't enough complete outfits to go around, and sizes were a problem, but every child had something, and Georgia, who was playing the march to open and was large for her age, had an entire dress. The rest of the clothes were apportioned: the tallest had skirts; the middle-sized bodices; the little ones what remained of the hats.

The hum from the front of the house had grown loud by the time some relic of the past had been secured to each performer and Martha led them, all on tiptoe, into the back parlor, where the furniture had been pushed against the wall and folding chairs were set, facing the hall. The children would go through the heavy velour curtains that hung between the two big rooms when their turns came to play or "entertain."

"No talking!" Martha warned them. "Absolute silence!" Esther would stay with them, to keep order and see that they got off according to the program.

Martha had to wait for over a minute when she appeared between the curtains, bowing carefully to the startled applause, then going to stand in the piano's curve until it subsided, her head to one side, its angle exaggerated by the tower of bonnets tied under her soft double chin. Once the room was quiet, she welcomed the parents and grandparents and old friends gathered there. She announced the march. She led Georgia forward. Again there was applause, and when at the second bar the procession appeared through the curtains, Esther at its head, swaying gracefully in the ivory satin wedding gown, the applause rose to such a volume that even with Georgia's foot stuck fast to the pedal the march was quite drowned out; the line of bonnets and bodices and skirts gave up keeping time and wandered. Down the length of the drawing room, between the audience and the piano, into the hall and out to the den, and so to the back parlor to enter the drawing room again—and again—and again. Every time Esther appeared, her cheeks pinker and pinker, the applause was renewed until Martha laid a hand on Georgia's shoulder, the concluding chords of the march were struck, and the last long skirt whisked into the hall, out of sight.

At intervals, Martha removed her top bonnet. By the final piece on the program, she had shown them all. She came on at the end with a flower in her hair—an artificial rose from Mama's going-away wedding bonnet—and David's locket suspended over the collar of black net. She and Esther wanted to thank them all for coming, she said, as indeed they wanted to thank the children for performing. She and Esther were so proud of the darling children. By now, the applause was tired. Martha acknowledged it. She knew they had sat long enough. But might she trespass on their patience another minute while they thought together of a friend now gone, though remembered perhaps by a few of those present—one who, like them, loved music and children and the art of speaking in public?

With dignity, Martha walked around behind the

piano and removed the lace curtain cut down to cover the picture of David that hung low over the exact center of the piano. A small picture, looking even smaller for the large mat that surrounded it. It would have been lost on the expanse of wall except for the American flag she had arranged over the top of the frame to lend it importance—and surely if David loved his church, he had loved his country as well. "David Rathbone," Martha pronounced in a round, full voice, and for a moment she pointed, unmoving, givng David his place in the afternoon. Then she lowered her arm, went back to the piano's curve, and bowed, to indicate that the recital was finally over.

Esther had come in from the back parlor for the unveiling. She stood at the far end of the front row, enough to the side that she could look both forward and back. She rested her hand on Oliver's shoulder. It was a protective gesture, but there was pride in it, too. She smiled, a little aloof, at the guests. Oliver smiled with her. He held up his hand for Esther to take, smiling and nodding in his courtly way, in a kind of approval, as if to say things had, after all, turned out for the best. And the children, released, wild to be free, rushed through the curtains to join their mothers and be off to the ice-cream parlor, for reward.

MY LITTLE SISTER and I marched in that parade—she in a bonnet with long, faded ribbons tied coquettishly under her chin, I in the puce-striped, leg-of-mutton-sleeved top of one of Emmeline Henderson's beautiful old dresses.

"Two gentlewomen fallen on evil days," was the way Mother explained it all to us, asking our forbearance.